Besmirched God

Besmirched God

Binay Pathak

PARTRIDGE
A Penguin Random House Company

ISBN: Hardcover   978-1-4828-1558-0
                Softcover   978-1-4828-1557-3
                Ebook   978-1-4828-1556-6

To order additional copies of this book, contact
Partridge India
000 800 10062 62
orders.india@partridgepublishing.com

www.partridgepublishing.com/india

To my parents

FOREWORD

'यत्र नार्यस्तु पूज्यन्ते, रमन्ते तत्र देवता:' (**The gods reside in places where women are worshiped**)

India is a country where women are revered from the bottom of heart from the time unmemorable. They are treated as deities. There is tradition to keep surname of women as Devi which means deity in Hindi and Sanskrit.

Ironically girls are killed in the womb, newly born girls are thrown away into dustbin. Females right from infancy to old age are raped brutally on one side and worshipped as mother and creator of universe on the other side. In conjugal life wives are treated inferior to husbands. Particularly in lower and middle class families women's plight is miserable. They have to bear atrocities from husbands and in-laws. Domestic violence both physical and mental is not new for women. In such circumstances if conjugal life continues it is only because wives forbear her insult otherwise most of the marriages were destined to be broken.

It is the story of a lower middle class girl Prabha who is beautiful and simple hearted. Due to dowry and other problems in negotiating marriage of a girl, her parents arranged her marriage at an early age. She has to bear with her snobbish, haughty and skeptic husband. Circumstances turn in such a way that she gets divorced even after giving birth to a son. No doubt her husband was totally responsible for it.

The setback of divorce is unbearable for her parents and they succumb to death one by one. Now she is alone in the world. One of the friends of her father helps her and she gets job on compassionate basis in place of her deceased father. For getting posting at her hometown she is pressurized to be physical with her boss. As she refused to do so she was posted at remote place.

She finds an amicable widower colleague in her office. Both are attracted towards each other. Prabha makes her mind up to marry with him finding him in the same condition she herself is. He is attracted towards her and agreeable to adopt her son too. But later she finds that he too is same skeptic person from his inner heart as her husband was and as a consequence she decides to live alone forever.

Listen to the pathetic story of Prabha from Prabha herself.

1

I was enjoying sun in the balcony of my house as it was very cold that day. After getting fresh and completing all household chores I cooked breakfast. I served breakfast to both Ajju and myself. We both have had breakfast. After that Ajju started meddling with his newly purchased mobile set and I sat in the balcony taking newspaper in my hand. It served dual purpose of glancing through newspaper and sunning myself. Generally I lie down after taking breakfast or meal on holidays for a few minutes and glance through some magazine. But the extreme low temperature compelled me to be in the sun. I was glancing through the newspaper when Ajju came in the balcony and asked—"mamma? Look here is Pradip uncle. I have got his number from your old telephone directory. I have fed all the numbers available on old and new directories and on your mobile set."

I looked at the screen of the mobile of Ajju. Yes! It was Pradip. His photograph was apparent on the screen of the mobile. His smiling face was looking very attractive.

"Mamma, I have fed all the numbers in the mobile and through an application photographs of all the persons who have smart phone may be visible on the mobile."—Saying so, he went inside the room and got occupied with his mobile set. Like his colleagues Ajju too preferred to stick to computer, TV and mobile set. Instead of playing outside in the stadium or sports ground boys today feel comfortable playing games on gadgets.

Two or three days before, I had purchased a smart phone on his incessant request. And from the day the mobile set had come in his hand he was every now and then busy searching and researching something or other on it. I was not aware at the time of purchasing this gazette that it will stir my mind, my soul vehemently in the same manner as a pebble thrown in the water of a pond swirls the water. But it did so . . . .

Pradip was the second man who had entered my life only after Viraj. The newspaper was in my hand and my eyes were on the letters of the news paper but down memory lane I was somewhere else. Seeing the image of Pradip on the mobile phone was just a disturbing factor for me. All the memories related to Pradip were passing one by one in my mind. And thereafter Viraj came in the picture. Again I recalled my childhood and my parents all one by one.

"Mamma I am going to my coaching centre."—Ajju was ready to go having bag on his shoulders and mobile set still in his hand—"Would you like to talk with Pradip uncle?" He asked enthusiastically.

"What is the need to talk to him? You go to your coaching centre. And why are you busy with mobile every now and then. I was not purchasing it as it would disturb your studies and you are not bothering for your studies and always busy with mobile set. Will mobile help you passing your engineering entrance exam?"—I scolded him.

"Don't worry mamma, I am just seeing what special features it has. It will never disturb my studies. As it is new I just want to be acquainted with all features present in it. I use it only after my study hours. I would certainly qualify engineering entrance exam."—Cajolingly he said and went out.

My mind was fully disturbed. I was here at Jaipur for more than five years. I had joined a commercial bank as an officer and was posted at different branches and offices in nearby locations. Here my world was limited in my home and office. Except Ajju no one was there in my life. The metropolitan culture had prevailed in the city and nobody was bothered with anyone. Neighbors seldom met and talked with one other.

After seeing the photograph of Pradip on Ajju's mobile set a curiosity raised in my mind to retrospect my life. I wanted to review all the moments of my life one by one. But the thoughts were congesting my mind and disrupting my thinking. Whenever I thought of one incident another intruded it and disrupted all.

Same was the condition once when I had seen a beggar beating his wife at Dumka, the place I was residing before coming to Jaipur. I was much disturbed at that time. I had noted down all the incidents in a notebook at that time. I had read that notebook several times but for last few years it was lying anywhere. If I get that notebook I will coherently retrospect my life. That notebook must have been in any of the bags. I would have lazed on other occasion but the tumult that was swirling in my mind did not allow me to be idle. I got the notebook after a frantic search in my divan. It was kept in a bag inside the divan. The notebook had become old. It was at least seven years old. Its pages were turned yellowish but it was quite readable. I started turning the pages. It was almost eighty to ninety pages. I was surprised how I could write such a long diary. Perhaps for soothing my mind at that time I would have written my autobiography. I lied down on the bed taking two pillows below my head and neck. I started reading the notebook one by one . . . .

While returning to my home from my son's school I stayed at a grocery shop to purchase onions as it has gone out of stock in my kitchen. I was way back home from St. John's school by a rickshaw. I asked the rickshaw puller to stop for a minute and went to grocery shop to purchase onions. There were a few shops on both sides of the road. Just after the cross road there was a petrol pump and on the other side of the road there was outskirt bus stand. Buses going to *Deoghar, Jamtara, dhanbad and Bhagalpur* stopped there for a while for passengers to get in the bus. Passengers were waiting for buses. There was a hotel in which some people were enjoying tea whereas others were having breakfast. The *halwai* was making *puri* and *jalebi*. The waiter was serving it to the customers. There was a betel shop in the corner. Some people were there for having cigarettes or betel whereas some were just for reading newspapers. Some people are very fond of newspapers but they prefer to read it at any betel shop or hair cutting saloon instead of purchasing at home. The shopkeepers find newspapers as attracter of customers so they allow people to read newspapers at their shop. Just between the hotel and betel shop there was a grocery shop. I was standing there waiting for the shopkeeper to weigh and pack onion for me. There I saw an ugly blind and handicapped person, clad in rags beating a dirty woman. He was shouting on the woman and abusing her very badly. He was slapping the woman mercilessly in between his uproarious abusing. The slaps were so strong and its sound was so resonating that I felt as if it were hit on my cheeks itself. He was asking very angrily—"where had you been for such a long time? How dare you leave me alone?"

The woman was crying bitterly. Tears brimmed her eyes and started flowing downwards and dropping on the ground gliding through his cheeks and touching her dirty *sari*. Some vagabond boys that were standing there without any purpose gossiping and bantering with one another were instigating the man—'what a brave man, a real he-man, bravo'. Hearing their voice the man got charged again and started slapping and buffeting the woman with full energy. And the woman was not moving from there to avoid the slaps and buffets.

"Where have you been for such a long time? I was shouting for you for hours"—the dirty grotesque man was repeating again and again. The woman was intact and stout so far as limbs were concerned. She was neither blind nor handicapped. She could have escaped very easily from there. And why think of escaping? She would have very easily beaten the man as the man was not only blind but also handicapped in one hand. But she was quite silent wiping tears in her eyes with one corner of her *sari*.

A gentleman present at the shop scolded the blind man—"O brutish man, why are you beating that poor lady?" He was a person of sound physique, tall and handsome. It seemed from his body shape that he was an athlete.

The blind man turned his neck guessing the sound and replied haughtily—"she is my wife, I can do with her whatever I like to do, and who are you to interfere in our affairs?"

Hearing this haughty reply from the blind man he went near him gazing at him very angrily. His gesture and posture was so bellicose that it seemed he would start thrashing him violently. The poor lady was watching this. She forgot crying. She realized that the man has got infuriated hearing arrogant remarks from her husband and he may beat him aggressively. So she came in between and asked the man requesting—"Please spare him *bhaiya* as he is a blind and handicapped person."

The man stared at the woman irately, as if he were saying how fool are you to save the person who has beaten you so mercilessly, returned from there on her request. He was unhappy to see that the woman whom he tried to protect is interested in protecting the bully. He picked the betel from betel shop paid the shopkeeper and went out muttering abuses for the blind beggar.

Watching such behavior of the woman I was surprised. The husband was blind, he was handicapped. He was totally dependent on his wife. He could not go anywhere without her help. Everywhere he needed help of his wife. And even then he beats his wife and his wife bears with him. He considers his wife his personal property with which he can do freely whatever he wanted to do. And nobody should get in his way doing whatever he wished.

In fact, they were beggar-couple and the woman escorted him from door to door to beg as it was not possible for a blind man to move freely. I had seen them many times earlier begging in the streets. They wandered almost everywhere in the town. I have seen them in my office area as well residence locality. Due to some reason, perhaps for lavatory, she was absent for a few minutes and husband started beating her brutally enquiring where she had gone for hours.

What was the reason behind the haughty behavior of the blind and handicapped man? This was because husbands are considered *Pati parmeshwer* (Husband, the God) in India. Whatever he does, in what so manner he does, is just right and it is obligatory for wife to accept his action however heinous, however cruel, however wicked it may be.

When I saw the grotesque faced dirty blind man beating his wife, my heart was full of anger and irritation. I wished I would have struck a strong slap on the cheeks of the man. But hearing the defensive plea from his poor wife I was astonished. What type of woman was she? She is rescuing the person who beat her so mercilessly.

By the way, I was getting late, so I collected the onion, paid the shopkeeper and boarded the rickshaw to go to home. In fact my son, Ajju, was a student in St. John's School *Dumka*. It was the month of July and as per rule of the school I had to deposit the fees of the school for the second quarter of the session. As *Ajju* was only seven, it was not justifiable to give him responsibility to deposit the fees; I myself went to school to deposit the fees. Had Pradip been available at station I would have requested him to deposit the fees and he would have completed the job very pleasantly as he always used to do so. But as he was out of station for some official work I had to go to school myself. While returning home from school I stopped at *Dudhani Tower chowk* to purchase onions. There I saw that unfortunate quarrel between the beggar husband and wife. I had to go to office by 10 o' clock and it was already eight. On the way to home on rickshaw I was thinking about the incident all the way. What is the condition of wives in our country? It is very miserable. May be some wives would have pleasant experience but most of them are nothing else but slaves of their husbands and in-laws.

Reaching home I cooked some food quickly, prepared Tiffin box for lunch and got ready and went to office. But the incident came abruptly during whole day in my mind every now and then. Even during office hour I was feeling sad over the incidence.

I returned home from office by 4 o'clock. Ajju too had returned by that time. He had some food and went out for playing in the ground with his friends. I prepared a cup of tea and started sipping it. Again the same scene was in front of my eyes.

In fact my sub conscious mind was correlating the incident with my own story. My husband was not blind like the dirty blind handicapped fellow that I saw in the morning but only to the physical extent. Mentally he was far more than a blind. He was not handicapped physically like that filthy person but mentally he was totally handicapped. It was not any other mental disease but only suspicion, skepticism and superiority complex of being a male, being a husband, being *pati parmeshwar, husband the god*. Today where he is I don't know. Neither have I wanted to know. I have not met him after he divorced me. But still there is true love for him in my heart. In fact he was my first love. In Indian society, particularly among upper caste, it is only and only husband who deserves love from his wife. For wife, husband is the first and foremost important man in the world. Although exceptions were prevalent in the past as is in present and is expected to increase manifold in future. But today my heart is filled with not only love. Hatred is in equal proportion. Truly speaking I can't say which emotion in my heart is dominant for him—love or hatred. Today I am divorced woman so I don't have any relation with Viraj but at the same time it is true that he was my first love and only love till the moment I decided to respond to his threat of divorce.

2

When I think about my life a strange hollowness envelops my mind. When I try to recall my early life I found myself a girl of about five. My father loved me much. I would not claim that he loved me much more than any other father of the world. But I know love for me in his heart was not less than the love of any father for her daughter in the world. I was the only offspring of my parents. Mine was a family which may be said both sole and joint. As my father was posted at Ranchi I lived there with him along with my mother. Family of my *chacha* (father's brother) lived in the village, *Krishanganj* about 150 kilometers from *Ranchi*. We often used to go to each other's home. Particularly during festivals like *holi-dussera* and marriage of relatives or other functions in the family of our relatives we used to go to our village and we all assembled and enjoyed with one another. My cousin-brothers and cousin-sisters liked to come to Ranchi as for them town was a matter of attraction. I too liked to go to my village as I found the atmosphere of the village very attractive and villagers very amicable and generous. As I was from a town my village friends respected me a lot. There was admiration in their hearts for me. As most of the girls in the village could not go to school and I was going to school I had a special place in their opinion.

Time was passing very pleasantly. In fact I never felt any type of dearth in the life. Who that is down needs fear no fall. I was low profile girl. My needs were very limited. I had no ego problem. I used to be mixed up very easily with everyone in my family and relatives. However I was introvert and felt uneasy in making friends with unknown persons out of my family or friend circle.

So far as study is concerned I was a blunt student and never expected much from myself. My father although wanted me to be a good student but seeing my attitude he became complacent ultimately regarding my student career. Anyhow I managed to pass the classes and that was much more for me.

Gradually I grew up in the company of my mother, father, uncle, aunt, maternal uncles, maternal aunts and all their children or my cousin brothers and sisters. Whenever I attended a marriage ceremony in neighborhoods or native village I could not stop myself from thinking of my own marriage. In my opinion marriage was a system in which wife and husband lived together. After marriage God manages to provide a child to the couple. Thereafter the family lives very happily and merrily. This was all that I thought about marriages and familial life.

In my childhood when I saw pictures of models of a suiting shirting company published in newspaper or magazines I used to tell my mother—"mamma, you must get such a handsome boy for my marriage.

My mother used to fondle my head affectionately and admonish lovingly—"my little girl, where are such boys in our caste? How can I select such a handsome boy when there are only few such boys in our caste?

"No, I need only such boy"—I used to get stubborn.

"Ok, Ok, first you grow up then I will ask your father to find such a handsome boy"—mother used to tell me.

In this way the life was going on. I was sixteen when I first appeared at matriculation exam. I failed in the exam and first time in my life I felt the need of serious study. Most of students in my school have passed and they got admission in colleges. This failure had depressed me. I had a chance to pass by appearing in compartmental exam but I did not want to pass with a patch, with a slender called compartmental or supplementary. At least what I heard people say about compartmental and supplementary examination. So I decided not to appear at compartmental exam and take the exam afresh next year. In my opinion it was better to pass a year later than pass with the help of compartmental exam.

I realized now why my father used to scold me to study seriously. Actually he had tried his best to enroll me in a good school for better education but I always managed to stay home anyhow. My grandmother was very helpful for me in this matter. She used to reprimand my father—"why are you always after my pretty girl? Is it good teasing the little girl that too for trivial matter like studying? Is study so important for a girl? Tell me, what is the use of study for a girl? A girl has to do household chores and bear and rear children. Is education so important to perform these duties? Most of the women in our family and cast are illiterate but can't they perform their domestic works efficiently. How can such a little girl go to a school that is so far from here? Don't dare irritating my fairy queen for trivial things like study."

As per culture of our family and our society and our country also my father was unable to speak a single word before my grandmother or his mother. Keeping in view the condition of female education by that time my grandmother was not wrong. At that time girls in small towns and villages were not expected to study seriously. Being capable of reading and writing was considered more than enough. After all girls were to bear and rear many children and do household chores and satisfy their husbands.

Thus by the grace of my grandmother I got liberty in studies and as a result marks obtained by me in matriculation exam was not worth telling anyone. The affection shown by my grandmother had not been good for me. But I could not complain against my grandmother for her blind affection towards me because she was no more. After favoring me and making my father reticent in regards to my studies she had passed away.

Now I decided that I would labor hard and will complete graduation with good marks. Or maybe this was a message from god that for getting a job after being divorced, education will be very important and helpful for me. That is what I think today. At that stage it was only reaction of failing matriculation exam.

I started my studies right from the next day. But as my base was very weak and even after studying very seriously and devoting lot of time I could manage to pass by a mediocre second class. Although it was an average performance I was very happy because for me, keeping in view my capability and my past record, it was a remarkable achievement. I did not expect more than simple pass. In fact I used to remember everything including mathematics in lieu of understanding it. And having such qualities passing by second class was not so bad.

I got admission in plus two in a local women's college. I was 17 at that time. Many new girls came in my contact in the college but being a reticent and introvert girl I befriended only two or three. There were much gossip among us but I could not understand all those gossips. As I pretended that I understood everything they started talking in code words now and then. Later when they came to know that I am quite unable to understand their covered gossips I was declared fool. Even my family members my elder cousin sisters declared me a child that knows nothing about life as per her age. In their opinion I had been grown up only physically and not mentally. Whenever I found younger girls playing *kit-kit* I started playing with them. I was then admonished by my colleagues or aunties living in vicinity—"now you are grown-up watch your body it does not befit such childlike play. You should not jump like this and you should put *dupatta* on your shoulder."

In the college I got a few new friends living in my locality. I used to go college by rickshaw, sometimes alone sometimes with one or two friends. I observed a few boys standing near our college gazing the girls and passing comments over them. I was quite unaware why they were standing there. Sometimes any of them passed comments on us too. I shared everything with my parents. So I talked about such peculiar behavior of the boys. They did not say anything specific in the matter but my mother advised me lovingly not to talk to these vagabond loafer boys and mind my studies. I obeyed my mother's advice and never paid attention to these boys.

"Mamma, I have to complete my homework"—suddenly Ajju came and opened the door with a bang. Hearing his voice I returned in the present from the past. I sat with Ajju on the study table. Ajju was doing his homework and asking my advice now and then. I helped him in completing his homework. After some time he started yawning and told that he would like to go to bed. I asked him to take meal first and then go to bed. I served him food quickly and went to bed with him. He started chattering various questions and his experience in school and playground on the day. Although I was replying his queries and talking to him, but mentally I was not present there. Ajju understood it and got irritated when my responses were not as per his expectation. But only after ten minutes he was fast asleep. After taking meal I too went to bed to sleep but I could not. The morning incident was behind me once again. Every now and then I recalled the scene—a handicapped husband beating his stout wife; strong wife being tortured by a weak husband. What was the reason? What was it that forced the powerful to be beaten by the fragile? Why the wife was bearing with the atrocities committed by the husband?

In fact it was not new in Indian culture. Most of the wives have to bear the nuisance of her husband. Even *Sita* faced the rude behavior from his husband *maryadapurushottam Ram*. *Ram* is the ideal of most of Hindus. Particularly he is ideal for devout *Hindus*. When their ideal icon relinquished his wife without any fault of her only on the basis of an allegation from a man how can we expect better deal from his followers and devotees. This was even when *Sita* was tested for her chastity giving *Agnipariksha*. Sita is known as incarnation of goddess, the mother and creator of the universe. When she had to bear such humiliation what can be said about a common woman. However many logic are being presented from the devout Hindus for this act of Ram yet the act of relinquishing one's wife is heinous crime in my opinion, whoever the person be committing such wicked act.

The same unfortunate life I had lived for almost three years. My husband, my first and last love, at least till then, had made my life so miserable that I would not like to live anymore in the word. Had I been issueless, I would have finished my life. But I had to live for Ajju, my only and lovely son.

3

Husband, was a beautiful thought for me at that time. Whenever there was any marriage in my native village I used to go there to attend the marriage ceremony with my parents. I found all the ceremony, rites and rituals and other things very interesting. The gathering of most of our relatives, near and far, was fascinating. We enjoyed these ceremonies much. The sonorous marriage songs and dances, *jhumar* and *chauhat* working and eating and bantering collectively, making merry with friends, relatives, boys and girls all was so pleasant, so lovely, so lively. When I could not go to attend a marriage due to my exam or other reason it seemed to me that I have missed something very special event. There was special performance in the night. *Dadi*, en elderly woman in the village, used to make different poses. Sometimes she dressed herself as a doctor and pretended to treat the patients. Sometimes she posed as if she were a saint and preached to the gatherings of ladies and girls. Her mimicry was so interesting, so lively that all burst into laughter. I recall one special act by her which is stored in my mind permanently. It creates enjoyment whenever I evoke the scene. On that particular day she feigned to be a doctor. She wore the pants and shirts of my father, took a bag in her hand and coiled a piece of rope around her neck as if it were a stethoscope. One girl asked her pointing a boy sleeping nearby on a cot—"Doctor *Sahib,* that boy has problem in the ear please cure it." *Dadi,* the doctor, went near the boy who was fast asleep even in that noisy atmosphere of marriage songs, bantering and laughter. She pretended to check the boy with her 'stethoscope'. "There is not a big problem; I will cure it in seconds"—Saying so, she brought her mouth near the ear of the boy and produced a trilling sound very loudly. The boy got up abruptly and saw here and there. There was a peculiar abstract on his face. He was totally confused. He could not understand at all what happened and what to do. All the girls and women were giggling seeing the reaction of the boy. The boy could not understand anything but as he was in the clutch of slumber so once again turned and slept as if there was nothing to react. Many such acts were being performed by *Dadi.* If she was absent due to some reason some other woman performed this task but no one could reach to the level of excellence at par with her in this job.

I recall one Kapil *Bhaiya.* He was son of sister of father of one of my cousin sisters in the village. He lived at *Pipli.* He was very jolly and lively person. He used to narrate different types of interesting stories how he managed in marriage ceremonies when some dire situation arrived . . . .

Once I was at *Hamirpur* to attend a marriage. People were taking meal sitting in a line and *daal (pulse,curry)* was not in desired quantity. There was a peculiar condition. What should be done? At least fifty people were sitting in the row enjoying food. Quantity of *daal* was not sufficient to be served again. What to do—uncle of the groom asked me. I suggested him a plan and he did according to the plan and the problem of quantity of daal was solved. How? Can you guess? Kapil bhaiya asked to the gathering around him very proudly. No one could tell the answer but watched his face curiously. "In fact"—*kapil bhaiya* started narrating the plan—"I had asked him to tell me loudly that there was a dead wall-lizard in the cauldron of daal. He did so. Hearing it I scolded him very vociferously—"what is the need to tell this incident so loudly. If the persons taking food would hear it would they like to take daal again? Just throw out the lizard from the cauldron and serve the daal." The people sitting in the feast had heard it because we both had talked so loudly intentionally to reach our voice to them. All refused to take daal when asked and the problem was solved in a minute. Ha . . . ha . . . . ha . . ." The people around him laughed whole heartedly hearing this interesting story of peculiar problem solving device.

It happened so in Hanumannagar that—Kapil Bahiya started another story—vegetable was not in sufficient quantity. More than fifty persons were waiting for their queue in the feast. What to do. I applied my mind. I just brought one kilogram of red chili powder and mixed it very well in the vegetable. It became too pungent to eat. The vegetable was served in paltry quantity to everyone in the first round. Whoever tasted it once did not dare to take twice. The problem was solved in a minute. Kapil bhaiya laughed whole heartedly and so laughed the people hearing his peculiar trick. In this way his story was ever lasting. His way of presentation was so interesting, so picturesque, so cheerful that everyone liked to hear it.

On one side group of old aged people were busy in religious stories . . . . Lord Shiva is so soft hearted that he did not distinguish between man and demon. Whoever worships him from the bottom of his heart he offers boon to him. Once he was trapped due to his simple behavior. It happened so that *Bhasmasur* made him please by his prayer and Shiva asked him for a boon. *Bhasmasur* asked him such a peculiar power in his hand that the person on whose head he keeps his hand would be charred. Lord Shiva provided him the boon and he tried to keep his hand on the head of Lord Shiva . . . .

On yet other side women were busy in their own gossip about relatives, about mothers-in laws and daughters-in laws and sisters-in-laws and about ornaments and about marriageable boys and girls and so on. Children were busy in playing *antarakshari* and so on.

Those were the days when I thought about my husband would-be. One day I too will be married. My father will search a suitable groom for me. Although the groom would not be very handsome, because in our caste, there are only a few such boys that are very handsome, yet my father will try his best to get a suitable match for me. Although I was not aware but heard from many that I was very beautiful. "You are at number one in all the girls in our family so far as beauty is concerned."—I had heard comments from many of our relatives, sisters, aunties and sisters-in-laws etc.

Out of dozens of cousin-sisters two were elder to me. Their fathers were in search of suitable boys.

One of these two cousins was daughter of my father's brother. She was *Nita didi*. The other was daughter of my mother's sister—*Swati Didi*. Suitable bridegrooms were being searched for both the girls. But there was no positive sign regarding settlement of marriage for any of them. One or other problem was deterrent in the way. Their parents were much worried for not getting a suitable match even after a long period.

There were or say are many problems in searching a suitable boy for a girl in India, particularly in lower middle class families. The first barricade is caste. Second barricade is sub caste. It is ironical that in some *castes* marriage may be performed only within a sub *caste* but in some *castes* marriage may be performed only out of sub-*caste* but within *caste*. You cannot marry outside the *caste*. Again there is *gotra* and *pur* and *shaakha* and many more. There are many types of *doshes* like *nari dosh* etc.. A *mangla* boy may marry only a *mangla* girl and so on. I have seen many cases in which it was rather difficult to find a groom for educated girls because educated boys are paltry in number in that *caste*. One such case is still in my office. *Kriti* is senior manager in my office. Although she can get many educated and employed boys for her match but as the marriage is bound to be within *caste* she has no option. She belongs to a lower caste family and very few persons from her caste are well educated or well employed. I have met his father Mr. *Amrendra*. How dynamic person he is, how lively, how enthusiastic his attitude is. He is ever pleasant. Even belonging to a lower caste he had reached a high position only by dint of his merit and labor. But he is unable to find a suitable match for his daughter. And the first and foremost reason for this is nothing but caste. A few families in his caste were there who could make progress.

Second hindrance is his confidant behavior. Families of boys never like self confident and egoist fathers of girls. They expect fathers of the girls to be timid and apprehensive. Rather they expect slave like attitude from them. How depressed he looks now. In fact he has to get her second daughter *Shruti* married too. The burden of marriage of two educated and employed daughters has squeezed the enthusiasm of his life. This is the plight of most of the persons who have marriageable daughter or daughters. Again daughter of one of my colleagues, Mr. Ramsharan, has completed MBBS course and become doctor in government hospital. Mr. Ramsharan goes every now and then to Rajasthan for settling marriage of his daughter. "Why do you go to Rajasthan for marriage negotiation, why not searching a boy here only"—My boss had asked him when he applied frequently for leave.

"Sir, There are very few people of the caste that I belong to here so I have to go to my native state for searching a suitable boy in my caste:—Mr. Ramsharan had replied.

Second problem is that of *Kundali*. In Indian society horoscope of both boys and girls are prepared and matched. The horoscope is prepared by *pundits* on the basis of birth place and time. There are so many conditions in matching the horoscope. Only a paltry 10 percent chance is there for perfect match of the horoscopes. God knows what the utility of this dogmatism is. It is believed that suitable match of kundali will lead to a happy married life of the couple. But I have seen a case of marriage in which the bride has turned widow within one month of her marriage. In this marriage bride was daughter of a horoscope specialist. The specialist claimed that horoscopes of both the bride and bridegroom were unique and he predicted cent per cent happy married life of his daughter and good fortune of his son in law. But it failed abruptly. Non detection of disease in time ended the life of the groom. Unique match of horoscope could not help the couple lead a happy conjugal life. What to talk about that particular marriage perhaps most of the marriages lead an unsatisfactory conjugal life of couple as except kundali nothing else is matched in our society. Neither education nor social strata nor any other matters like likes and dislikes of the couple. May be such marriages would have a success in old days when marriage was considered purely a religious affair. But in today's circumstances conception of marriage has been totally changed. It is not now religious affair but a social and contractual affair.

Dowry is another giant hindrance in the match for marriage in Indian society. Due to this problem many beautiful and virtuous girls remain unmarried in our society whereas ugly and useless incompetent girls not only get married but also get comparatively very good and able boys as their husbands, so far as look, quality and income is concerned. The boys and their families forget everything for want of dowry. Otherwise what may be the other reason for a matured good looking person marrying an ugly, inept girl? In fact it is only to get some hundreds of thousands of rupees and assets in dowry. Perhaps these boys are mentally handicapped. Otherwise why should they accept such girls as life partner for few thousand rupees? Even if a progressive educated boy objects this system he is being suppressed by his parents and other family members emotionally and he is constrained to accept their belief. In some of areas of *Bihar* boys are being kidnapped for marriage. The relatives of girl kidnap the boy, perform marriage rituals and send the boy along with the girl. The boy has to accept the girl ultimately. This is established practice in some families. God knows how such type marriages succeed.

Although there is one act against dowry in India yet the ubiquitous and strong coils of dowry system has not spared anyone including people from police, administration and judicial. Of course nothing related to dowry is kept in black and white in marriage negotiations to avoid harassment by law.

There are some such cases too where relatives of brides misuse the dowry law. Bridegroom and his family members have been tortured by brides and their families.

There are many such acts in India which are restricted in the books of law only. Dowry act is one of them. Indians are very ahead in making laws. So many laws are there in country in every field and ironically lawlessness is prevalent everywhere. Laws and acts relating to consumers are perhaps the biggest one in India but what is the position of consumers, everyone knows. This is the country where milk is being prepared from detergent and urea. This is the country where restricted medicine is sold unrestrictedly. This is the country where grains, sweets all contain cancerous elements. This is the country where spiritual *babas* are doing heinous crimes like rape with minors. This is the country where top leaders are indulged in bribery and other heinous scams and remain out of clutch of law.

So my cousin sisters *Nita didi* and *Swati didi* were burden on their parents as there was not only problem in getting a suitable boy but it was too costly as dowry and other costs were to be met. *Nita didi* lived in a small town and being twenty one years of age was not a matter of much worry as there was an understanding, in comparatively literate towns, that child marriage should be avoided. But *Swati didi* lived in village. She too was twenty one. But as per prevalent marriage practice in the villages the age of twenty one was considered much more for marriage of a girl. There was an all accepted opinion that early marriage is better, particularly in case of girls it was much widely accepted fact that girls should be married earlier.

The long hands of law are unable to eradicate child marriage completely. In many child marriage cases grooms have turned vagabond whereas brides turned well educated. How an educated girl can accept a tramp or truant her life partner? But they have to do so in the name of tradition, society, culture and other things. Even today such incidents are common. But in few cases brides have out rightly denied to accept the marriage that was performed in early childhood, at the stage when they were not able to understand even the meaning of marriage. However such girls have to face many problems from village community.

In such circumstances there was much hue and cry in the village for *Swati didi's* marriage getting late.

Experiencing the problem of getting a suitable boy, particularly in case of Nita didi and Swati didi, my parents decided to start searching for a suitable boy for me. As per their calculation it would take at least three to four years in finding a suitable groom and by that time my graduation would have been completed and I would be in the range of twenty one-twenty two years. As I was living in Ranchi, which was comparatively a big town, this age would not irrationally high for marriage as per the standard fixed by the society.

4

My parents discussed with some of their friends and relatives about my marriage. Some educated people expressed their disagreement on marriage in such an early age. Some became very happy with my parents for taking such a pragmatic and timely decision. One of my neighbors *Ganesh chacha* lived at *Sitanagar* as he was posted there. He used to come from Sitanagar on irregular intervals, in a month or so. On hearing about planning of marriage they suggested one boy who was an assistant in State government Department. His relative was posted at *Sitanagar* and was neighbor of *Ganesh Chacha there. Sabita chachi,* wife of Ganesh *chacha,* was a good friend of the wife of boy's relative. She collected all related information like horoscope, photo etc from her neighbor and provided it to my parents. Horoscopes were matched and it was a good match as per *pundits.* The first obstruction in negotiation was fortunately over. My father went to the village of boy's father for marriage negotiation.

His father easily agreed for the marriage. There was a whim of happiness among all our family members. All were very happy. Even Nita didi and Swati didi along with their family members were very happy—at least as it looked so apparently. Later I learnt that there was an indignant murmuring among Nita didi's family and Swati didi's family about my marriage. In their opinion there must be something wrong in the groom or groom's family. Only then the marriage was settled so easily. In fact they were jealous of my as well as my parent's good luck. They were surprised how a marriage can be settled so easily. It was more surprising as the boy was employed in State Government service. Some parents were frantically searching grooms for their girls for more than four to five years. They could not succeed in getting a suitable match. So they were very jealousy of my fortune, although they tried their best, albeit unsuccessfully, to hide their ill emotions.

But there was a setback in this. Later boy's father has put his demand for dowry in such a way that it was rather impossible for my father to fulfill it. Boy's father has given a list of demand to my father. In fact his demand was worth Rupees 300 thousand. It was a big amount those days. This amount was rather impossible for my father. It appeared that marriage negotiation had failed because their demand would not be met on any cost. My emotions were hurt terribly. I was feeling very poignant. In fact from the day the marriage had been agreed I had admitted it from the bottom of my heart as my in-laws house. I had accepted the boy as my husband at the core of my heart. Although I had learned that he was ten years older than me yet I had no objection or problem. Because in India husband is treated as god and perhaps it happens only in India. Whatsoever demerits he possesses, how unfit he may be he is to be revered, to be worshiped, to be adulated.

A photograph of Viraj was obtained from his father for showing to my mother and relatives. It was kept in the cupboard. Whenever some of our friends and relatives arrived at our home the photograph was shown to them. When someone gave nice comment seeing the photograph my parents became very happy.

I used to watch the photograph of Viraj whenever there was no one present around. He had a photogenic face. He looked smart in photograph. Although I had heard discussing members of my family that he was not good looking. As he was going to be member of our family so it was remarked as 'not good looking'. The inherent meaning was that he was ugly. His physique was like an old man and his face was black colored and grotesque. When he laughed he looked like an old thin man. It appeared that a cartoon has been animated by an expert. His gait too was like an old man. He walked stooping his shoulder. I had heard some of our relatives talking about him. I asked my father one day—"papa, how he looks? Is he a boy or a man" Papa just replied—"he is Okay and is a matured man." No appreciation from him confirmed that he had any feature which may be praised.

Being an adolescent I did not like to hear it. In fact I wanted a boy for my match and not an elderly man. But what could I do? In Indian lower medium income group society girls are not supposed to interfere in their own marriages. At least by that time it was so. May be situation would have changed a little bit. They had to accept whatever their parents and elders had decided for her. Same is the situation in twenty first century except in few modern families of high society. Particularly in upper caste families it was very strict practice. I have seen so many girls in my village who were married with old aged, completely bald, squint, humped back, even insane fellow. No one had refused to marry such person. What to talk about refusing no one even expressed her dislike openly. Such girls simply shared their disappointment with their intimate friends blaming their own fate, cursing their own luck. In such circumstances it was not astonishing that I accepted it without any resistance and later on, my heart, my mind and my soul has accepted him as my life mate, as my savior, as my god, as *pati parmeshwar* (husband the god).

Later on my marriage was settled finally. In fact it was not the father of the boy who was desirous of dowry. It was one of his wise and sensible relatives who had put such a huge demand on his behalf. Viraj's father had just read out the demands. Later on when he was asked about the financial problems faced by my father he accepted the amount that my father offered.

Thus my marriage was settled finally.

5

Preparation of marriage was on full swing. Initially the venue for the marriage was considered at Krishnaganj, my native village but later it was decided to be performed at Ranchi itself. All close relatives have come one week before the marriage day. I was much happy in the company of Nita didi and Swati didi. We were doing shopping for marriage, doing rites and rituals and formalities of marriage, enjoying everything.

It was matter of great pleasure for my parents. They thanked god for solving their problem of fixing marriage of a girl so easily and so quickly. In fact Nita di and Swati di were elder to me. Their parents were searching a suitable boy for their daughters for years. Even after four years they were unable to find a suitable match. In many cases they did not like the boy and his family and in many cases where they found the boy and family both acceptable, demands from groom side was not satiable as some of them wanted lots of money and jewelry and property in dowry whereas others wanted highly educated girl in specialized field. Others were in search of miss world or miss universe like bride. Such was the case with the families demanding lots of money were not well off themselves. Families demanding highly educated girl have not a single educated girl in their family. Again families demanding miss world or miss universe like bride had not a single woman in their family that can be called even good looking what to talk about beautiful. But as they were from groom side they were free to put their demand how ridiculous it may be considering their own status. In such circumstances my parents were much happy and thankful to God for getting a suitable match for their daughter.

When Nita di and Swati di got free time they made fun of me. One day when we were on siesta after mid day meal, Nita di told me smilingly "Don't resist if your husband try to remove your clothes, and allow him do whatever he wants to do on the first night."

I was stunned listening this. What is she saying? Why any sensible man will do so? "How dare he would do so, what are you talking"—I screamed

"Stupid now you are grown up, why don't you understand anything?' Swati di scolded me." It happens between wife and husband; did not you watch such things in movies? Have not your heard the song "Suhagraat hai ghunghat utha rahaa hoo . . . ." When he will remove your clothes and . . . ."

"Mamma, mamma . . . ."—I cried resenting their imprudent gossip.

My mother entered the room quickly and nervously. "What happened, Prabha?"—She questioned.

"Look both Nita di and Swati di are talking very dirty things to me"—I complained to my mother.

Mamma understood the situation and advised me smilingly—"learn something from elder cousin sisters. Now you are going to be married. You must know what you are expected to know as a married girl otherwise your husband will suffer and will resent your ignorance."

I was surprised with mamma's such advise. I thought she would enquire into the matter and reprimand both Nita di and Swati di. But to the contrary she was advising me only to learn something from my cousin sisters. What to learn from my elder sisters? Removing clothes of a person? O my God.

Date of *Tilak* ceremony was fixed. In fact on this day family members, particularly male members from bride side, go to the residence of the groom and perform some rituals. Dowry in cash and kind is provided in the hands of groom. This sacrament is to be performed by brother of the bride. As I had no real brother one of my cousin brothers performed this ritual. This ceremony had a great success. Everyone was very happy. The persons who went in Tilak ceremony were appreciating groom, his relatives and his house. When the boy is employed his physical appearance is not important, nor is his age. Groom side had given warm welcome to all and arranged a grand ceremony.

Just after three days of *Tilak* ceremony marriage day was fixed. In between there were some small rites and rituals every day like *Madapachchhaadan* and *Gritadhaari* etc. In mandapachhadan bride sits under the mandap along with her parents and some rituals are performed. Elders bless the bride. They offer turmeric and sandal paste to the bride with their blessing. Again there is great bantering among the persons. They apply paste of turmeric and sandal on each other's face.

All the functions were being performed with great zeal and enthusiasm. All were rejoicing the functions. Many of our relatives had met after a long time. They all were taking news and views of each other. There were much talks and gossip among them. Exchange of ideas and information about marriageable boys and girls was the most important issue amongst all. I and my parents sat many times under *mandap* and *punditji* performed many rituals. He pronounced hymns very loudly and sonorously. I could not understand what he was uttering in Sanskrit but performed all the rituals as he directed. Many times a day *ubatan* was applied in my entire body by ladies who were in relation my grandmothers and aunts, paternal and maternal, elder cousin sisters and other ladies of the village. During applying *ubtan* they sang epithalamiums in very melodious voices. Although none of them was a good and professional singer yet the songs appeared very solacing to my ear. I have heard these songs many times before and I liked it always but sitting under *mandap* as a *dulhan* it was far more appealing. The words of some of the song were very stirring—"Father why are you exiling me, Uncle, why are your exiling me, grandfather, why are . . . . , brother . . . ."

Am I going to be exiled? I thought. No, all these are matter of saying. It is Just a marriage song and nothing at all. I am just going to another home. My father has found a good husband and family for me. No other father is able to do such a job in such a little time. There is nothing like exile here. Although my parents would not be present there yet my parents-in—laws would be there to substitute my parents. Again my husband will be there to take care of me.

On the day of marriage I was wearing red coloured *lehanga* and *choli*. I was told by Nita di and Swati di that I was looking very beautiful. I think they were expressing very honestly what they were feeling. There was not any taunting or formality in their expressions. In fact I had seen abstracts of praise in the eyes of everyone present there. I could not stop myself to look my image in the mirror. Seeing myself in mirror my cheeks just flushed. Really I was looking very beautiful in bridal dress.

Viraj came with *barat* to my well painted and decorated house. There was very attractive fire cracking from groom side. All the neighbors were very much impressed with light, *band party* and firecrackers. All the persons from the house of the alley were watching the *barat* from the roof of their houses. I and Viraj both sat on a magnificently decorated colorful cushioned chairs hired from tent house which were meant for such purposes and occasions. We exchanged garlands as per tradition. It is called *varmala* or *jaimala*. I saw Viraj first time in my life. Same was the condition with him. Although we both had watched each other's photograph earlier we were seeing each other physically first time. When we were standing face to face taking garlands there was much applause from audience.

'Don't bend down Viraj, let *bhabhiji* manage to garland you"—Viraj's friend were screaming in excitement. Viraj smiled in response and remained straight for some time. It was difficult to put garland in his head due to this. After all he was taller than me at least by six inches and it was difficult for me to put the garland in his neck. Again I was wearing heavy dress and ornaments. At the same time I was very nervous too. Ladies from my side persuaded him to bow down his head so that garlanding may be performed. But he refused smilingly. There was much amusement. I was feeling nervous. I could not understand what I should do. Ultimately Viraj bowed his head and I could garland him. There was a great thunder of clapping. Thereafter he too garlanded me. It was easy for him as I was short heighted. Again there was euphoria of applauding. After *Jaimala* ceremony I returned into my room and Viraj went to *janawasa*. My friends were asking me question like did you like you hubby etc. *Muhurt* for marriage was between 2.00 A.M. to 5 A.M.

At 2.00 A.M. Viraj was called to my home along with a few of his close family members. In fact both bride and bridegroom sit under *mandap* and *pundit* instructs to perform rituals to bride, bridegroom and parents of bridegroom there. Parents of bride and other persons remain present there. People from groom's side may be present there If they want.

Only after a few hours I observed that Viraj is looking resentful. He was not performing the rituals with good mood. In fact he was performing all the jobs asked by *pundit* half heartedly. I could not understand at that time what the reason behind it was. Seeing his unwillingness everybody became aware that he is not happy with the marriage. But what may be the reason? He was well aware about everything in the marriage negotiation. He never told anyone anything in the matter. He never put any demand nor did he give any instructions regarding marriage. Then why there was resentment on his part and for what and with whom?

The next morning there were lots of traditional formalities like *majalis, barnet, pairpuji* etc. After completing these formalities on the day I had to go with Viraj to his home as per prevalent tradition. There was much hue and cry in my home as it used to be and still uses to be in the bride's home on the day of departure to the house of in-laws. My parents were just weeping from the bottom of their heart but for my sake they pretended to be okay. It is perpetual story on the *bidai* day in the house of Indian brides. On the day of *bidai* brides shed tears as they have to depart from their parents' home and go to quite hitherto unknown family. Parents also feel very sad as they have to send *their lovingly* daughters away from them. These were the daughters, whom they brought up very affectionately, right from their birth to the present. Although marriage is considered to be a boon in Indian society yet on the day of *bidai* everyone virtually whimpers in brides' family. However life becomes normal only after that day and everyone adjusts accordingly.

It is a prevalent and very popular jest that brides weep only on the day of *bidai* but bridegrooms have to weep for life thereafter as he has to obey his wife whole life. This is the matter of jest but fact is that brides weep on *bidai* day overtly and on rest of life covertly. At least that is what I think and women whose fortune is unfortunately like that of mine would definitely agree with me.

6

When I reached my in-laws house although there apparently seemed zeal and enthusiasm yet Viraj's behavior during the marriage ceremony was much talked there. There was murmuring that Viraj did not like his bride that is me. But even his family members were not aware for what reason he did not like the bride. In fact his relatives had asked him earlier to see the girl before marriage negotiation but at that time he had denied to see the girl. Viraj was getting double minded at that time. On one side he was showing complete faith in his family's choice on the other side he wanted a girl of his choice and what was his choice perhaps he himself was not aware of. His family members had selected me for the marriage. But now he was showing his dislike towards me. What was the reason I could not understand then. But now I think that in Indian society, particularly in middle class family, it is very easy to get married but very tough to get rid of marriage. Only a few persons in high political circle or show-business were exercising right to divorce. Perhaps every groom in the middle class society feels him to be out of demand in the society after marriage.

Viraj's subconscious mind was saying him that after marriage he would be no more in demand in girls' family-circle as he used to be before marriage. And perhaps in his subconscious mind I was the main reason to blame for this downgrading so far as Viraj' life was concerned. That is what I think today contemplating over the subject very deeply and I don't claim that what I think is perfect or true. It may be one reason or one of the reasons or may not be so. May this reason upset a groom or may it be quite ineffective on other. It is true that not all the persons after marriage behave in the way Viraj behaved.

When we met at our first night he behaved like a sex-starved person. He did not wait for anything and just prepared himself for sex. At that time his dislike towards me was nowhere apparent. On the other hand I was quite unknown and unaware about sexuality. The only knowledge in this regard that I had was Nita di's and Swati di's suggestion—"don't resist if your husband try to remove your clothes, and allow him to do whatever he wants to do . . ." And I just did so albeit very reluctantly.

After a few minutes he was fast asleep. He was snoring very loudly. It was very difficult for me to sleep. Again there was a peculiar unpleasant smell oozing from his body. I wished I could be far off this stench. His snoring was so sound that it disturbed me. I could sleep very late that night due to these problems. Whenever I was sleepy his snoring changed track and its irritating sound did not allow me to sleep.

Early in the morning there was a knock on the door. I got up and opened the door. "*Chachi* has asked you to take bath earlier there is *satyanarayan puja* and *punditji* would come for it. Please convey it to *bhaiya* also."—One girl asked me. Perhaps she was a little girl from Viraj's close relatives. I awoke Viraj. He yawned and a queer smell emanated from his mouth. It was disgusting. But I was not supposed to tell him anything about it otherwise he would have resented. I told him the message received from the girl. He got up and went out for getting fresh.

Puja started. Punditji prepared *gobar ganesh* and performed all the rituals, blew the conch after each lesson and narrated the parable. Whole day was spent in doing various rituals and meeting relatives and neighbors.

In the night when Viraj came in the room he asked me—"had you have illicit relationship with anyone?—His face and voice was overfilled with doubt.

I was stunned by this question. I did not want to reply this stupid question, but I replied—"no and never"

"Then someone must have molested you taking in confidence"—He retorted like a great psychologist.

"What are you saying; it's completely wrong and baseless". I kept my voice as strong as I could but I was not supposed to scream in my in-laws house that too the very second day or my arrival, as I was a newly married bride. What an ironical situation it was. On one side bride is quite unaware about sexual activity and on the other side bridegroom is blaming her for illicit relation. This was height of skepticism.

But he never believed me. He always suspected me for the crime I had never committed. What was the basis for his suspicion I could not make it out. This suspicion was the first gift that was given by him on the occasion of *munhdikhai* which is considered a very important and religious value in Indian society. When anyone sees first time the face of his bride he presents her some gift. This tradition has special meaning for husband when he sees the face of the bride first time or unveils her veil at first night. What I received on that occasion was just this distrust, doubt, disbelief.

He told me that he hated me and did not want to live with me. I was not surprised hearing it as I had watched his behavior in marriage rituals. But when he said that in Europe and America and other advanced countries couple depart by taking divorce when they do not like each other and he wished he could do so, I was shocked. Just the second day of marriage I was proposed for divorce. I got perplexed. I was worried not only for me but for my parents too. In fact I was more worried for my parents rather than for myself. I was afraid that even hearing such matter would shock them ruthlessly and there heart would break. They would not afford tolerate this shock.

"When should we get divorced then?" Asked Viraj

"My parents have great expectation for our successful and happy marriage. For their shake it should be deferred for at least a few years."-I replied gloomily. Although I wanted to say that what is the need of divorce. I would adapt the qualities that you expect from me. But why I could not say so, I don't know; I can't say.

"Okay! Two years will be appropriate?"—Viraj proposed.

I nodded my head in affirmation. I could not speak anything. Happy moments experienced by my parents on the confirmation of marriage negotiation and during marriage ceremony flashed in my mind. How would they feel when they would come across such proposal? But who is going to say them about it. At least I would not reveal it. Their happiness must continue till it may be continued.

I could not understand what the reason behind his behavior was. Every now and then he blamed me for illicit relations with someone or other. I tried to make him understand that there is nothing like that but my words could not succeed to convince him. I swore by the name of God and my parents but all in vain.

I was very talkative from my very childhood. I used to talk to him about everything and every person even after his allegations and blames. Whenever there was a reference of a boy or man he correlated me with that boy or man. In fact he was mentally sick in this regard. What was the basis of his nasty thinking I could not understand but this skepticism was just hurting my heart and soul. I was feeling very gloomy about his dismal behavior. Every time I talked about any boy or man his bases for blaming me just increased.

"Once I went to attend the marriage of daughter of my mother's sister at Harinagar. There one of their neighbors Satish was friend of son of my mother's sister. As he was very close family friend he every now and then came in the house. Seeing me he exclaimed how beautiful this girl is. From where has she come?"—I was just chatting with Viraj.

"Then there must be some hidden story that you are not telling me. Let me know the entire story. What happened thereafter"—Viraj just remarked.

"What hidden story?"—I was surprised but soon realized what he wants to indicate.

In this way whenever I talked with him and there was a boy or man in the discussion he just correlated that boy or man with me. I was just fed up with his behavior.

I was very busy there as guests and relatives came every now and then and I had to go before them to show my face I could not put much attention to his words. After three days I had to return to my parent's home. My father came along with my one cousin brother to take me home back. It is tradition in our society that bride returns her parent's home after a short stay at in-laws house and thereafter second marriage called *gawna* or *dwiragaman* is performed after some time and bride again goes to in—laws house and thereafter she can freely live at in-laws home and return to parent's home for a short period as per requirement and will. Perhaps this tradition commenced because in ancient times marriage was performed at very early age. And early marriage was because India was infested by invaders who used to lift unmarried girls with them. To protect girls from the invaders early marriage system started and now it had become time tested tradition and there were a few deviations in it. This was residual of old marriage system when child marriage was prevalent and bridegroom went to in-laws only after she was fully grown up and after stay of a short period she used to return to her parent's home.

While departing from there, my father invited Viraj to come with us. He flatly and haughtily refused—"no, I have much work to do." It was apparent from his response that he does not care for the feelings of his wife nor of his father in law.

7

I returned from In-laws' home with my father and cousin brother. My mother, friends and all asked me about my experience, about my stay at in-laws, house. I narrated them a few goods things experienced there. But I could not tell anyone anything about the behavior of my husband, the god, rather the besmirched God. It was the god whom I loved much and who had very special place in my heart but who besmirched his own reputation by his own behavior, by his own attitude, by his own acts.

But I could not be able to conceal my experience to my mother. Perhaps she was expecting something wrong keeping in view the behavior of Viraj during marriage rites. Or she was able to read my inner gloomy face which was masqueraded by a happy and jolly face.

"Is there anything wrong between you and your husband Prabha?"—My mother asked when we were alone in the house.

"No, mamma, nothing is wrong."—I tried to make my face and voice as normal as I could so that she could not know my predicament.

"Don't tell a lie to me. It is clearly written on your face that you are not happy with your husband. What is the matter? Tell me the truth.—Mamma asked me straightforward.

I could not conceal the fact. I narrated my mother—"mamma he is skeptic, he every now and then blames me for illicit relations. It seems that he doesn't like me."—I narrated to mamma.

"Don't worry. Such nature is common in men. The only thing you have to do is to bear everything silently. With the passage of time everything will be correct."—Mamma advised me.

Although I was now busy in daily routine yet I always recalled Viraj and moments spent in my in-laws' house. I was not expecting Viraj to come because I knew that he hated me. But I was wrong. I forgot one thing. He hated only me and not my body. His sex desire did not allow his ego to stay there. He came on the next Saturday evening. There was a pleasant excitement in my family. My parents were very happy on his arrival. It appeared that there was a great occasion, a great festival. Viraj was welcomed very warmly by my parents. If I say that I was not happy it would be absolutely wrong. In fact I too was very happy. I thought that all problems prevalent in Viraj's mind have been solved so he had come to meet me. After all I was his wife and there must be feeling of love for me in his heart. He lived with us for two days. He was very lovely and amicable during first day of his stay. His mood was very jolly. But he did not forget to tease me every now and then—"someone must have molested you or you had relations with someone. I know it." Although he said so in humorous tone but it was apparent that the bugs of suspicion have not vacated his brain. Only on second day he returned to his original mood. In fact one of our acquaintances Harish uncle invited us with family. This was just to welcome Viraj. Harish uncle was colleague of my father and he was just like our family member. He treated me like his own daughter. We all went to their house. They warmly welcomed Viraj and us all. The entire Gupta family was very lively and talkative. They were very humorous and shared many pleasant moments and cracked jokes. As there was very close relation among our family they were talking informally with us. God knows why Viraj did not like all this. He presumed that he is being insulted by Gupta family, that too in our presence. Although he did not react there overtly but later his mood was off. He stared me angrily. He stopped talking with me. I asked him time and again—"what went wrong?"

But he kept silent most of time. The words he uttered were—"I don't like all this" But he did not clarify what he did not like, what went wrong.

The next morning he was lying on the bed with remorse mood. I was sitting on the bed beside him. "What happened?"—I asked

There was no response. He just turned his face to the other side.

"Have I committed any mistake"—I wailed.

"Not you, I have committee mistake. By marrying girl like you"—he growled.

"If you will not let me know what is my mistake how can I rectify it?"—I said remorsefully

"You need not rectify anything. Just leave me alone."—He rumbled.

I put my hand gently on his body. He just threw it off and grumbled—"just leave me alone."

His mood went worse when some of friends and relatives came to meet him hearing about his arrival. When I asked him to come in drawing room to meet our family friends and relatives he remarked—"Am I a zoo animal that you want to show me to your friends and relatives?"

I had no reply of this question. It is common in small towns and villages that people of acquaintance come to the house of each other, particularly on such occasion when newly married son in law comes first time.

After two days he returned to his place of work. He used to write letter to me almost daily. On weekend he came to meet me. I was not supposed to go with him until my second-marriage (*gawna*) as per prevalent tradition. His letters were very fantastic. It appeared that a clean hearted and open minded litterateur has written it. I was much happy. I thought that the differences between us are only because we are from different families and it must be sorted out completely very soon. I showed the letter to one of my very close friends *Lata* as she had many times requested me to narrate my experiences with my husband and also to show the letters of my husband. Due to hesitation I never shared with her my personal moments with Viraj but showed her the letters received from Viraj. She too was very much impressed by his letters. She praised the style and expression of Viraj—"it seems that a great learned has written the letter. Is he a student of literature?"

"No! He is a science graduate."—I replied.

"Then it is even more important. A science graduate is writing such a ornamental letter. You are very lucky to get such a husband."—Lata told.

"Alas! I wish it would have been so"—I mumbled.

When Viraj came next time I told him very enthusiastically about the appreciation of his letter from *Lata*. I was expecting that he would be very happy hearing it. But to the contrary, he became red with anger—"how dare you show my personal letters to anybody? I had written it for you and not for anyone else. You are not worth to be written. I will never write to you." Although he was right yet in my opinion it was not such a big issue. I vowed not to show his letters to anyone in future. But he did not forgive me. This incidence was more than sufficient for making him resentful for which he always remained in search of a reason. The whole Sunday his mood remained off. I was repenting why did I tell him about the letter. Rather I was regretful for showing the letters to Lata. I should not have shown our personal letters to anyone. On Monday morning he returned without saying a single word to me.

This was not a single instance. Every now and then he got an issue for resenting and most of the time he stayed annoyed with me. My every sentence created adverse effect on him even if I spoke in his favor, cajoling him, persuading him. In this way he used to quarrel with me on this or that ground.

At one occasion he was angry with me for some reason. I said—"You are senior to me in age, should not you forgive me for my faults?" He just got angry—"You mean say that I am an old person? Who said you to marry an old person? I had not come to you with marriage proposal."

Most of women wear *sari* after marriage in our society. Particularly in village married women do not wear anything other than *sari*-blouse. I too used to wear sari after marriage. But many married woman in town and cities used to wear *salwar-kurta occasionally.* I have heard that ladies in metro city even wear jeans trouser and top after marriage. I had many *salwar-kurtas* which I used to wear before marriage. Most of them were in good condition. Particularly those *salwar-kurtas* which were purchased in recent one or two years back were in very good condition. I just put on one day *salwar-kurta.* I felt salwar kurta very comfortable, very easy than *sari* as I put on *sari* rarely before my marriage and that too for one hour or two on special occasions. The next Sunday when Viraj came, saw me in *salwar-kurta.* This was a solid ground for him to get angry."

"You just did not want to marry me that is why you are dressed up like an unmarried girl." He put his allegation. I cited many examples where married girls were putting on *salwar-kurta* and even in jeans and T-shirt. But no arguments were to get him convinced.

In this way for this reason or for that reason he remained irritated with me. I could not make it out what was the reason behind his behavior. If he wanted supremacy then it had already with him as in middle class society in India wives consider themselves inferior to their husbands. I was not exception to it. Like all women I too considered him everything of my life. But perhaps he wanted this feeling taken to be granted and only for this he behaved in such a way.

I often thought why wives are considered inferior to their husbands. There should be parity in the relationship of husband and wife. But why husbands are considered Gods and wives are treated as slaves? Perhaps it was due to two reasons. First wives are wholly dependent on husband as they have no independent source of income and no ownership on wealth. Secondly in so called high caste society a wife cannot get rid of his husband in her lifetime. How cruel the husband be, how incompetent the husband be, wife is not supposed to be free from him. Even after death of husband she cannot marry again. Thanks to various social reformers like *Raja Ram Mohan Ray* and British government that *sati pratha* had been eradicated from this country. How cruelly wives were being immolated with the dead body of their husbands. Even today many widows are forced to live deserted life. They are not supposed to participate in any of the auspicious ceremonies in the family. Many widows from Hindu family take shelter in religious places like Brindavan as they have been deserted by their family members, by their sons, whom she brought into being. There they lead a life of beggar even having profound property. Perhaps this was the reason that wives in middle class upper caste family lived a life of second class citizen and were considered not better than a bonded slaves or dismal animals.

There is story of *Sati Savitri* who had saved her husband from the clutch of *Yamaraj*, the god of death. But there is no story where husband had saved his wife. To the contrary woman had been cursed by his husband when someone molested her making guise of her husband. Women have been cursed by their husbands for no fault of them. During partition the women who were lost from their family and met after a month or two were never accepted by their family members on the ground of their robbed off chestity.

There are many festivals like *Teej* and *Karwa Chauth* for women who aspire for long life of their husbands keeping fast for whole day without any morsel of food or single drop of water. But there is no such festival for husbands. They do not need to aspire for long life of wives. Wives are nothing more than a baggage for them which may be replaced if one is lost.

8

Most horrible days were yet to come for me. After passing twelfth class I took admission for three-year degree course. It was my dream to be a graduate. In the meantime my *gawna* (second time arrival at in-laws house) was completed. I went to my in-laws home second time and after short stay of a week returned as I had to stay at Ranchi for my classes. Viraj had no problem in my staying at Ranchi until he was not aware of my intention of completing graduation course. But as soon as he came to know that I am doing my graduation and for that stay at Ranchi is a must, he changed his attitude. He wanted me to be with him at *Rampur* where he was posted. In fact he was more interested in disturbing me rather than living with me. By disturbing me his ego of being husband, being superior would be satisfied. I requested him to let me live at Ranchi at least for those few days when my classes were on. But all went in vain. He was not ready to allow me to stay at Ranchi.

I had surrendered to him every time earlier when there was a bickering between us. Nay, not when there was a bickering between us but whenever he thrashed me for one reason or another. But this time I could not capitulate. A graduation was my greatest dream or the only dream of my life. The day I had failed my matriculation exam I had sworn that I would complete my graduation at any cost. Although I did not want to upset my hubby, the god, rather besmirched god, yet it was not possible for me, for my heart, for my soul to quit the ambition of graduation. I was quite helpless in this matter as my conscious did not allow me to relinquish my well awaited and the only aspiration. I promised him that as and when the college remains closed I would be with him at *Rampur*. And colleges here remain closed for more than six month in a year. There are so many grounds like summer vacation, *various Pujas like Holi, Dipawali, Dussera, Eid, Bakrid, Gurupurnima, Budh purnima, Mahavir Jayanti*, Christmas day celebrations, New Year celebrations etc. For entire May and June there is summer vacation. During October-November the classes remain suspended continuously for festivals like Durga Puja, Deepawali and Chhath. Colleges remain closed on last week of December and first week of January every year in the name of Christmas day and New Year celebrations. There were other many bases on which colleges remain closed for a long duration. But Viraj was not ready to hear anything. My parents first tried to convince Viraj for allowing me continue my studies, but due to his stubborn attitude they advised me to postpone the idea of graduation. My parents, particularly my mother tried to persuade me to relinquish the idea of graduation—"What is the use of graduation? Why we teach our girls. We do so only because there should be convenience in settling marriage of the girl. You are lucky that your marriage had been settled so easily. See the condition of your cousin sisters. Now you have to manage your home and rear children. There is no use of doing graduation."

But I was this time disobedient to my parents, perhaps very first time in my life, to accept their advice.

Viraj used to come at Ranchi on Saturday and return on Monday. He came sometimes on other holidays too. He was adamant to take me to Rampur and I was not ready to leave my college classes. When I asked him to take me to Rampur during vacation he flatly refused saying that he would accept it only if I would completely give up the idea of doing graduation and live with him permanently. God knows why he was after my ambition of graduation.

In between I came to know that I was pregnant. This was another shock for me. It was shock for me because I was not ready for this before completing my studies. Otherwise being pregnant is considered as a boon for a married girl. Just after a few months of marriage relatives expect news like this. There are traditions like *godbharai* in which there are pleasant functions on the occasion of being conceived. Women who are unable to bear child are considered unfortunate in our society. Even seeing the face of such women in the morning is considered ominous in our culture. But for me it was nothing other than a shock because I did not want baby for the time being as I had to complete my studies first. I opted for abortion. But as usual Viraj was against it. He was opposing the idea of abortion not because of any particular reason. The only reason was that I wanted abortion and he had to oppose it as being husband, being male he was supposed to suppress me, my ideas, my views, my ambitions, everything related to me. My parents were also against my idea. They illustrated many examples where abortion of first baby had spoiled the life of would be mother as she could not conceive later or conceived with great difficulty and hectic treatment and adulation to many gods and deities. They also assured me that they would help in rearing the child and I would never be disturbed in my studies. Thus the idea of abortion was aborted and I had to play role of mother along with the role of student.

During summer vacation I offered Viraj to take me Rampur for two months. But he did not accept my proposal. He insisted on quitting my idea of graduation.

"Why for two months only? If you really want to be with me you will have to live with me permanently and forget about college and graduation and all that"-he put his rationale.

"Please try to understand, I will live permanently with you anywhere you wish but for god's sake let me complete my education, it is only matter of few years. It is my only dream. Even in between I will be with you on all vacations and holidays.—I implored.

"What is the use of education for you? I will never allow you to do a job. You have just to do household chores for whole life. For cooking food and cleaning utensils and sweeping and cleaning up floor there is no need of graduation or post graduation or FRCS. Then why are you adamant for completing graduation"— Viraj growled.

"How could I make you understand? I am always and will always with you. I love you, I adore you. You are God for me. You will ever be god for me. I request you to please let me complete my graduation, I will never ask for doing job. I am not interested in doing job at all; I just want to complete my graduation. After completing graduation I will confine myself completely in household chores."—I reiterated.

"Had you so interested in doing graduation you should have done it before marriage. Otherwise you should have deferred your marriage. At least I would have escaped the misfortune of marrying and living with you."—He took shelter to sophistry.

He never accepted my request. When he could not put any rationale for stopping me from study he just started to harass me by other means. To the contrary he every now and then accused me of illicit extra marital relations. He put allegation on me that I didn't want to continue conjugal life with him.

"You must have illicit relation with someone that is the reason why you don't want to live with me and with the rider of graduation course you just want to enjoy with your beaus"—one day Viraj told me.

"Why are you saying so? What to talk of illicit relation I had never talked to any man outside my family. I have no time for such heinous jobs. I am busy in household chores and studies only. Such illicit relations are not found in families like ours. These things are only in cheap novels and films. Such incidents may be in families like yours." I said in anger.

He became furious hearing my words. His eyes got red with anger. His face became rigid. He looked at me as if he would swallow me up.

"don't befool me. I know you have illicit relations and that too not with one but with many. You are bearing me only to show the society"—Viraj growled angrily.

This continued for many weeks. I was so disturbed that neither I could do household chores well nor concentrate on studies. I used to open the book and study but could not understand anything. My mind was always intrigued with Viraj's allegations. I was one who never knew about sexuality before marriage. After marriage Viraj's behavior was so inappropriate for a novice girl like me that I never enjoyed sex. I was just an inert partner in this regard. How could I have extra marital relations with anyone when I had no interest in sex? And I was accused of extra marital relations by my husband, the god, the besmirched god. The god, who had immense reverence in my heart, just smirched his own reputation by his obscene allegations and filthy behavior.

My brain started dizzying. My soul screamed. What should I do? Should I kill this rascal Viraj who is smirching my character or should I kill myself and end this predicament. All these tensions and worries would finish with me. But is killing self or any other person so easy? Had it been so easy perhaps I would have committed it long ago. Again what would the condition of my parents? And what will be my reputation like? Killing of a husband or suicide is in itself a big factor for people to spread nasty rumors. The people would decipher it in the same way as Viraj had hitherto blamed me. His blame will turn in reality in the opinion of the world. I was in a fix. My baby was developing in my womb. I had learnt that pregnant women should be always happy because her mental status affects the baby. I have heard a story about *Lord Buddha*. A woman along with his five year old son went to *Buddha* and asked him what to do to teach her son in a good and effective manner. Buddha replied that there was inordinate delay as babies should be taught right from the period when it was conceived in the womb. Again there is a story that *Abhimanyu* son of *Arjun* had learnt the art of entering labyrinth only when it was in the womb. He had heard talk of his parents while in womb and learnt the skill. He just could not learn to come out of the labyrinth because the moment *Arjuna* was narrating it to his wife *Subhadra* she fell asleep.

So for baby's sake I wanted always to be happy. But neither I, nor my baby, was fortunate enough to be happy in this situation. The days were passing by gloomily in this way. It was not so that Viraj always remained in same nasty mood. Sometimes he appeared to be a very good husband and an excellent would-be father. But such mood was very rare.

9

Month of December was very crucial for me. In fact doctor had advised the delivery that during last week of December to week of January. As my annual exams were expected in the month of March, I was much in tension. On one side I had to prepare hard for the ensuing exam on the other side due to last stage of pregnancy I could not concentrate on my studies. And the mental agony provided by Viraj was everlasting.

On 27th December 1997 Ajju was born in a local hospital at Ranchi. I had to stay at hospital for two days. Viraj had not arrived from Rampur as the baby was expected in the first week of January as per doctor's latest advice. After two days I was discharged from the hospital and I returned home. Although I did not want baby before completion of my studies yet I was very happy seeing Ajju. In fact I had very pleasurable feelings seeing the little angel. I felt that I am creator of an excellent, wonderful and most beautiful infant in the world. I had read that being a mother is a beautiful feeling. I realized it is really so rather it is the most beautiful experience. I cannot explain in words the pleasure that I felt.

Viraj came to Ranchi the next Saturday. He too was very happy seeing Ajju. Most of the time, he was busy watching the baby. It seemed that he is watching the most beautiful and most attractive thing in the world. His eyes stuck to the baby's face for several minutes. He observed each and every expression on baby's face. He used to sing joyfully taking little Ajju in his arm. He talked with the baby very pleasantly unaware of the fact that the baby was too little to understand his talk or respond to it. Sometimes he touched his tiny hand again and again and kissed it. Sometimes he fondled the cheek of the baby. He talked to Ajju lispingly like a baby. The pleasant expression on his face was something spectacular.

It seemed that Viraj has changed. Ajju's presence had changed him completely. His frowning face was transformed. A piquant smile was apparent on his face. He talked with everyone including myself very congenially. I was much happier. It was on the one side due to the newly born baby and on the other side due to the skeptical and cynic husband turned pleasant and jolly.

There was a ceremony called *Chhathi*. It is celebrated on the sixth day after the birth of the baby. All our friends and relatives were invited on this auspicious and hilarious occasion. As Ajju was the first grandson of my parents, there was a great celebration. We all enjoyed it. Parents, Brothers and sisters of Viraj have also come. During these days Viraj was very happy and cordial. There was no sign of his usual cynic behavior. I thought all my miseries have gone forever.

After two days all the relatives returned their home. Viraj too was back to Rampur. My studies had been hampered badly as during delivery period and chhathi celebrations there was no chance or time to study.

I once again tried to concentrate on my studies as there were only a few weeks left in starting of exam. But my motherly duty for Ajju was deterring my studies and at the same time it was being deterred by my studies. My duties had become tougher despite most of the household chores and baby related works were completed by my mother.

Viraj was coming on every Saturday as usual. After a small gap of his generosity he had again converted in his original skeptic form. He every now and then taunted on my studies. He blamed me of illicit relations as usual. Now he had one more reason for quarreling with me. He blamed me of shirking my motherly duty. One day he crossed all his limits when he blamed that Ajju is not his son. He is only his nominal father. His biological father is someone else. In his words his biological father was one of my beaus for whom I was staying at Ranchi in the name of studies and not going with Viraj.

Although every time he blamed me of illicit relations I was mentally shattered and shocked vehemently but his verbal attack was increasing day by day. He had to compensate all the dues of blaming me that was missing after Ajju's birth and *chhathi* celebrations. Now it was enough. Rather more than enough. I was not in a situation to bear his nasty and spiteful, false and baseless allegations. When during showering his obscene allegation he wished to divorce me I could not keep mum as usual this time.

"Better I would not have married you; I want to get rid of you. I want to divorce you"—Viraj uttered with disgust. He would have screamed very loudly. But as my parents were present in the room nearby and there was possibility of his voice reach them he uttered chewing the words.

I was very upset at that time and replied firmly—"If you want to divorce me I am ready for it. You can divorce me. I am also fed up with this hellish life and your brutal false and baseless allegations."

Hearing it Viraj was stunned. Perhaps he did not expect such a straightforward reply from me. He has taken my endurance for granted. He was sure that whatever behavior he will show I would never oppose. In fact I too did not want to reply in such a way but his accusations had crossed all the limits and boundaries and it was unbearable now for me. My reply was just spur-of-the-moment.

It was Sunday evening. He did not talk to me thereafter. When I served him dinner at night he ate up silently and did not utter a single word. He did not take Ajju in his lap. He slept with me on the same bed but did not talk to me at all. It was first time in my short married life that sleeping on the same bed he abstained from having sex due to resentment. Before this too he had quarreled with me many times. But on bed he was unable to remember those quarrels and started making love, albeit after some minutes or hours later. Whenever he fell in the clutch of slumber he put his hand on my waist but as soon as he realized it he drew back his hand. I was feeling very weak. Although I had replied him in anger but I did not mean it very seriously. Divorce was not meant for families like ours. My parents were quite unaware of this development.

On Monday he got up early in the morning as usual. Getting ready he left for bus stand to go to Rampur. He did not speak a word to me. Nor did he cuddle sleeping Ajju as usual while departing for bus stand. He went to Rampur. Although my parents understood that he is resentful for some reason or other and there is some misunderstanding between us but as it was quite usual and routine matter for him and consistent with his behavior, they did not take much care of it. They thought that after a few days the situation would normalize as usual.

I was in a fix. On one side I was very much grieved by the verbal abuse of Viraj and on the other hand I was worried for my parents. If they would know about the quarrel between us they would be very unhappy. Particularly my mother will be very angry with me as she incessantly used to expound me to bear with husband and keep quiet when he was in anger. I could not understand what I should do at this juncture.

The days were passing. I was awaiting a letter from Viraj. In fact many time he returned to Rampur getting angry with me but the next day he used to write letter to me which reached me two or three days later. His letters were so full of emotions that I would forget all the bickering with him. There were just two personalities he possessed. When he was with me he was skeptical and cynic and very abusive. But whenever he was away from me he appeared very wise, sensible and sympathetic. At least it was so what his letters revealed about his personality. So I was very anxiously waiting for his letter. In fact due to the quarrel that we had last week I could not concentrate on anything. I was not studying properly. Neither could I do household chores well nor was I able to attend to Ajju properly.

Next Saturday I was waiting for evening right from the time I awoke. I was waiting for evening, because Viraj used to arrive in the evening. He used to leave Rampur at 2 in afternoon by bus and reached Ranchi by 7 p m. It seemed that the day has become very long. Every second appeared to be greater than an epoch. It was seven in the evening. Whenever I heard the sound of plying of Rickshaw I thought that Viraj would have come. I used to go to veranda to see whether he had appeared. But each time I was disappointed. The clock struck eight . . . then nine . . . and then ten. There was no any chance of Viraj coming now. It was because if he missed last bus from Rampur he used to go to Harinagar and took bus from there. In such case he used to reach by 9 at night. As it was already ten now, there was no chance anymore for his arrival. There was a great tussle between my brain and heart. My brain was saying that Viraj will not come but my heart expected his arrival. My brain analyzed the last week event and arrived at conclusion that as Viraj was hurt he would not come. But my heart said that Viraj should come. After all I was his wife. He had not seen Ajju for more than five days. The love for Ajju will force him to come. My brain was applying rational whereas my heart was applying emotion. My parents were also waiting for him ignorant of the episode that occurred between us last Sunday.

"May be there would be extra work in the office so he did not come today"—my father opined.

"It may be so."—My mother replied; she was quite ignorant about our quarrel.

I was aware of the situation but could not tell anything to my parents.

"Your papa could not come today due to extra work"—my mother was talking with little Ajju stammering like a little baby touching his cheeks affectionately who was lying in the cradle beside the sofa quite innocently moving his hands and feet.

"He will come tomorrow and love you. He will bring toys for you"—my mother was talking to Ajju tickling his stomach. Ajju got enthused hearing the voice of my mother and started smiling and moving his hands and feet faster.

I knew that this time Viraj has got hurt, he will not come tomorrow. I was worried. My eyes were full of tears. My mother watched me and consoled me—"due to some official or personal problem, Viraj could not have come. Why are you shading tears? It is quite natural for a serviceman to stay at office due to workload."

"No mamma, it is not the problem due to which he had not come. In fact he had got angry with me and only for that reason he had not come"—I told sobbingly.

"What happened between you both? Tell me the truth."—My mom questioned in utter surprise.

"Mamma, he was blaming me as usual for illicit relations with some boys. He even told that he was not the father of Ajju. Instead he was Ajju's only nominal father. His biological father is someone else. He wished he would not have married me. He was asking for divorce. I too said in anger that I was ready for divorce if he wanted so."—I narrated the situation to mom.

"Why did you do so? You should have tolerated and kept mum. In our society wives do not argue with husband. It may spoil your life"—My mother repeated the teachings that she used to deliver whenever she saw signs of resentment on Viraj's countenance.

"But it has become unbearable now mom. Did not you watch his behavior? He blames me every now and then. I have never thought of illicit relations with anyone. Even then I have to hear the heinous allegations. I could not stop myself when he blamed that Ajju is someone else's son"—I submitted to mom.

"You should not have done so in any circumstance." My mom told. There was a deep expression of anxiety on her face.

10

There was much tension in the hearts of all in my house. The only unconcerned was little Ajju because he was in the golden stage of his life. Perhaps it is the only stage in the life when one is tension free and even if there is a tension someone other has to tackle the problem. My mother asked my father to write a letter to viraj. My father too considered it apt in the situation. What would have been the consequences, had my father not written the letter to Viraj, I can't guess. But this letter perhaps produced adverse effect. Viraj became haughtier when he received and read the letter. Before next Saturday his reply was received—"I don't want to live with the girl I don't like. I just want divorce and Prabha too wants so. She has expressed her intention clearly to me. I am ready to pay half of my salary, rather two third of my salary but can't live with her."

My parents hitherto considered it normal bickering between wife and husband. In their opinion it was common between newly married couples. They were expecting that on next Saturday Viraj will come. Their assumption was not quite baseless. In fact during last 15 to 18 months we wife-husband had quarreled several times. Rather Viraj has resented several times for this or that reason. I had been just a silent subjugated. He had stopped talking with me many times. On many occasions he had stopped writing letters to me. On a few occasion he had not come on Saturdays that was followed by quarrel between us. So my parents thought it was same story again and they were hoping situation to be normalized soon.

But my heart was saying that Viraj would not come now. I had never opposed him so strongly before. His super ego was hurt due to my unexpected and abrupt behavior this time. My words "I too am agreeable for divorce if you aspire so" had caused a permanent negative effect on his evil heart.

Viraj did not come on next Saturday too. Although I was repenting to some extent for my behavior towards Viraj yet I was adamant this time not to bow down because I was not on wrong side as usual. He had been not only blaming me for many months but he had replied my father's letter very haughtily. If god has decided divorce in my fate then let it be. There are many women in the society who have been abandoned by their husbands. By surrendering to heinous attitude of husband it may be possible to avoid abandonment but what about widowhood? It is not in the hand of any person. This is matter of destiny. There are many women who have been widowed and who have to live alone in the world. It would be better to live alone than to be abused and maltreated every moment by an egoist, haughty, boorish and brutish husband.

It was 3rd March 1998; I recollect very well, I was studying in veranda though not very attentively as my mind was intrigued in difficult situation.

"Postman"—a voice attracted my attention. I lifted my head hearing this word toward the voice. The postman was coming inside opening the gate. There must be a registered letter—I thought—otherwise he used to throw letters on the floor inside boundary only from there. My heart blossomed like a flower expecting letter from Viraj. But he never used to send registered letter. I was again disappointed recalling this. There may be ordinary letter along with registered letter. I gave assurance to myself. Perhaps his anger has been pacified I expected. Postman came near me and handed over an envelope and asked me to put my signature in token of acknowledgement. There was only one envelope. This was not a letter from Viraj. I recognize his handwriting very well. I signed on the sheet provided by the postman and opened the envelope. This was a notice from lawyer. Viraj had opted for divorce. Perhaps I should have wept for it but god knows why I became more rigid than before. Only before the moment I was very happy expecting a letter from Viraj. But now I was in different mood. If he wants divorce then it is okay. It will be very difficult to live alone in present society, but was it less painful to live with such a cynic husband? His heinous allegations not only shattered my heart but my soul also. It would be perhaps more apt to end my life at this moment. But ending of life originates many rumors in the society. Most of the rumors are unfavorable for a woman. Particularly character of a woman is very fragile in our society . . . there must be something wrong with the woman otherwise why should she commit suicide . . . she must have entangled with someone etc. etc. Again how could I commit suicide leaving my little beloved son Ajju. At present I am breastfeeding him. Again his father will perhaps not keep any relation with him after my suicide. Then who will take care of him. No doubt my parents loved him much. They will try their best to rear him in best possible way. But they are themselves old aged. How long they can take care of him. And what would be their plight if I commit suicide. No, it is not pragmatic idea. I just threw away this negative idea. Again is it easy to commit suicide. Perhaps it is not. Thinking about it is something other but acting is quite different.

There was much hue and cry in my house. My father started to teach me—"such trivial bickering are common among wife and husband. There is quarrel and bickering between every couple. But the matter should not go to such an extent. You should never talk about divorce. You can't understand how destructive it may be for both of you and for Ajju also. Reputation of our family as well as Viraj's family will be tarnished in the society. No such case has occurred in our near and far relatives. What to talk of relatives such practice is not prevalent in our caste, in our country. These things are prevalent in western society or among *bollywood* people because for them marriage is nothing more than a play, a contract. We firmly believe that marriage is fixed by god in heaven. No one has right to disobey the decision of god."

My mother was very much angry with me. She was crying on me—"You must have committed some blunder. You must have insulted him. What is the use of your education when you do not know how to talk and behave with your husband? Go with your father to him very tomorrow and apologize to him."

For a moment I became weak. I thought I should apologize. It has caused much tension in my family. How gloomy my parents have become. If I apologize the problem would be sorted out and my parents would become satisfied. But soon I recovered and became determined as I recalled all those bad memoirs with Viraj. I said straightforward to my mom—"I would never apologize to him as I have never committed any mistake. It is he who insults me every now and then, every moment. I have endured all his atrocities without any resistance. But now it is enough. If he wants divorce, I am ready for it. It is better to live alone, to live a divorced life, to live a widowed life rather than to live with a cynic and skeptic person. If you will force me anymore I would hang myself."

Hearing my words my mother was shocked. She stopped crying. She could not understand how to manage the situation. In her opinion I should have cried at this juncture but there was a rigidity on may face. Reading it she could not speak anything.

My parents wrote letter to parents of Viraj regarding this hoping some positive result. Needless to say that my parents apologized on behalf of me in advance assuming that there was fault on my part. In fact divorce was a slander in a lower middle income group rustic *Brahmin* family. Viraj's parents too endeavored tirelessly to convince him for abstaining from such an impractical decision. They too were of the view that trivial bickering between wife and husband should not come to such a destructive end. This would be a slander on the family as no such incidence has taken place in the family in the past. But Viraj was not ready to listen to anyone—neither his own parents nor mine.

In Indian society particularly at that time it would not be easy to get divorce if anyone of the spouses opposed it. But in my case I was not to oppose. As we both were agreeable for divorce the judge approved it after two or three hearings. I can't say whether Viraj had bribed the court personnel for favorable and early judgment or not but I was now divorced woman. There was an order to pay half of salary to me in judgment order. Just after one or two days after our marriage Viraj had proposed for divorce, though not very firmly. I had requested at that time to defer it for some time as it would have been a great setback for my parents and he had fixed two years for it and incidentally time turned in such a way that just after two years we were divorced.

11

It was not less than death or even more ferocious than that for my parents. All relatives and friends were asking the reason of our divorce. They could not reply the baffling queries of their friends and relatives. People who felt jealous when my marriage was finalized were now very zealous after my divorce. 'Haste makes waste; hurry spoils the curry'—they were sharing with each other—'It is not so difficult to negotiate a marriage but we do not want to negotiate such a fragile marriage. It is better late finding everlasting marriage than settling such early marriage which ends in a divorce. What a slander! Divorce is not a fate of marriage in an honorable and prestigious family; it is not acceptable in our holy country. It is not tolerable in the country of *Rama, Krishna, Buddha and Gandhi* etc. etc.' Most of our friends and all the relatives have almost broken relation with our family. For them our divorce was only a topic for delicious gossip and nothing else.

I was quite unable to understand whether to be happy or sad. My married life could not see even third anniversary. It was pitiable for me but on the other hand I was free from the cruel atrocities and heinous allegations that have turned my life into horrible hell. Was not it a cause for rejoice? But frankly speaking I was very much in depression over this incidence. No doubt I too chose the path of divorce but it was affecting my mental and physical health. I was not able to concentrate on anything. Sometimes I thought that I have taken a wrong track.

All our near relatives were very much upset with the divorce. It was now like a slur for them to be our relatives. They had just forgotten us. Even the persons who were obliged by my father and who boasted of being our relatives started ignoring us. Now we were confined to ourselves. Only colleagues of my father and our neighbors were there with whom our family had contacts. Although many of them saw us with suspicion in their eyes they did not discard us totally.

Ajju had become one year old now. His father never took notice of him. Viraj's family was also now alien for him. His grandparents did not ask for him. It is said that interest is dearer than principal. Many times people ignored their son but not grandson. But here the case was different. His paternal grandparents were of the opinion that it was Viraj who was link in the chain of our relationship. As Viraj had absented himself from the chain of relation so there was no question of continuing relationship with us. For Ajju there were only three persons in the world who cared for him—me and both my parents.

My parents had become like dead bodies. All the pleasures and happiness were meaningless for them now. My father remained busy in the office so he could bear this setback to some extent but my mother was losing her health day by day. Although she did not blame me directly yet her eyes were telling that she was very angry with me and it was I who spoiled everything. As she had to see me and Ajju all the day she could not recover from the trauma and one morning when I found that she had not got up even late in the morning I went into her room to awaken her. But perhaps she had slept with an intention of never getting up. My father could not realize this. He was glancing through newspaper in the verandah. Hearing my scream he entered into the room. When he saw my mother lying dead on the bed the disappointment that was spread over his face was not easy to describe.

For thirteen days the house was full of guests and friends as rites last for thirteen days. Many of our relatives avoided to come even on this occasion. Many came just to complete formality as they were of the thought that whether one attends happy occasions or not one must attend sorrowful occasions. People were counting it second great inauspicious incident in our family. The first one was obviously my divorce.

With the divorce the relation between families of mine and Viraj's had vanished but my father had posted invitation card to Viraj's parents also to come on my mother's funeral rites. No body from there came to attend the rituals.

Now Ajju had lost one of the most loving persons in the world. I had to care for entire household chores along with caring Ajju. My father tried to help me but his mental position was not stable. Again he was accustomed to neither household chores nor rearing child. My mother had managed house so well that he was never worried to look after these things. He tried to keep him busy with Ajju. But his eyes were always in search of someone in the house. But it was never ending pursuit.

My father, who looked normal until death of my mother, was losing his confidence. It seemed that my mother was attracting him from the heaven right from the day she died. Within six months she was able to attract my father completely. Feeling pain in the chest he was admitted to the hospital. Harish uncle, colleague of my father and neighbor of ours managed to take him to Dhanvantari hospital. He returned home only when not only the pain was over but even throbbing of his heart had stopped completely. That day I got a peculiar promotion. Now I was not only divorced but orphan too—orphaned divorcee or divorced orphan. Alas God! Do not give such misfortune to anyone in the world, not even to my greatest enemy or ill wisher.

I was alone now in the sense that no one was there in my family who would give me support. There was no use trying to find assistance from relatives. To the contrary I alone had to look after the little Ajju. The alimony that was fixed by court in the judgment of divorce suit had never given to me and god knows why I did not care for it except when after death of my father I was in need of money. But by the god's grace and Harish uncle's help I received quick aid from department of my father and was not compelled to take shelter to maintenance allowance fixed by the court.

In our society a divorced or widowed woman is quite vulnerable. Particularly woman like me are unfortunate who had none to support or protect. Neighbors or relatives that seemed to be very helpful and supportive after my parent's death were in fact having ulterior intention. Price for their help was something very costly; not from economic point of view but ethical point of view. In fact they wanted me to be physical with them in consideration of their help. Although no one proposed it overtly yet their intention was quite clear. So it was better not to take any help from them. Among them Harish uncle was of course odd man out who helped me in getting job on compassionate ground in place of my father. He always had fatherly love and affection for me. His true fatherly love was proved when even after my being orphaned he helped me without any hope of return. He spent much time and money for completing formality for my job. It was he and his family who supported and protected me.

It would be better for me had I got the job at Ranchi itself. But the director of the department wanted me to understand the problem faced by him in posting me at Ranchi. And he wanted me alone in his bedroom to make me understand and that too preferably at night. One day when I was in his office for completing some formalities he asked me to come at his residence for a format was not available at office and it was available at his home. I went to his residence. There his servants welcomed me and took Ajju to his lawn where a beautiful hammock was there. They were entertaining Ajju and offering him biscuits and chocolates. One of servants brought tea for me. Director came and sat there. He told me that his wife has gone out of station. He clearly told me the price fixed by him for posting me at Ranchi. I was stunned. For this reason he had called me at his residence in the name of form. I was disgusted at his behavior. He was of the age of my father. I asked him irritably "how you can talk with me in such a way.

You are like my father and I am daughter of a deceased employee of your department."

"Be practical! For getting posting at Ranchi itself you will have to pay some price. Otherwise you may be posted at remote place and it will be difficult for you to live in unknown town because you are quite alone."—He told sternly—"And don't talk about father and daughter like relationship, There are many facets of relation, look at one"—Saying so he forwarded a newspaper to me. I glanced through the heading. "Father raped his own daughter for several years"-The heading was printed in extra bold and big letters. I just threw the paper in front of him, came outside the drawing room and took Ajju from the hammock and came out of the boundary of that rascal's house.

Harish uncle had said me that it is the director only who can decide my posting. He every now and then advised me to pray to the director for local posting. Perhaps he was not aware of the condition that the director had stipulated for my posting at Ranchi. I too did not tell him anything as there was hesitation in my heart to talk such matters with him as I always treated him like my father. Harish uncle could not do anything in this matter because in bureaucratic set up he was too junior employee to talk with the director. I was not ready to accept director's heinous proposal. In fact it was not and never in my nature. No matter I had been blamed for such a character by my ex husband. So I did not get my posting at Ranchi. The director sir deployed me at Dumka, the second capital of Jharkhand. Perhaps it was the remotest place in Jharkhand where our office was located and he posted me there. After delaying to the maximum possible period he gave me the appointment letter. However it took almost two years. However pension was paid to me regularly and it helped me in my subsistence.

I arrived at Dumka after getting appointment letter. The bus started at seven in the evening and reached at seven in the morning. Although the distance was not more than three hundred kilometers yet due to dilapidated condition of road the journey was very hectic. As it was only seven in the morning and office time was ten it was problematic to spend three hours. So I stayed at a hotel. The hotel was near the bus stand. It was not very good hotel yet it was counted among the best hotel in Dumka as Dumka was not very developed town by that time. I got fresh. After taking breakfast I went to office by 10 o clock. Ajju was with me. There I met the head of the department, Mr. Prasad. He was a person of above fifty years as was evident from his graying hairs and slight wrinkles on his cheeks. He asked me to take my seat and called his orderly by ringing the bell. Orderly came in and waited for his order. Mr. Prasad was asking me the formal questions like domicile, education etc. He expressed sorrow knowing the fate of my marriage and demise of my parents. He was feeling the agony and sorrow that I faced and did not enquire deeply regarding my divorced life. He asked the orderly to bring two cups of tea and a good chocolate.

"Dumka is a very peaceful place. You may live very peacefully at this place. Although it is not comparable with your home town Ranchi so far as facilities are concerned yet everything is available here for a middle class citizen to lead an easy life."—Mr. Prasad continued talking.

"Sir, my first requirement is a secure house and second a house maid who can see may son when I am in office. No one else is there to live with me."—I said to him politely

The orderly had come taking two cups of tea in a tray and a chocolate. He gently kept the cups of the tea on the table one before me and another before Mr. Prasad and handed over the chocolate to Ajju. Mr. Prasad offered me to take tea by indicating towards the cup and lifted one himself. Ajju tried to unwrap the chocolate but when he could not succeed gave it to me to unwrap. I opened the wrapper of the chocolate and gave it to him. He started munching it.

"There is one house in vicinity. Mr. Pradip will tell you about the locality"—Mr. Prasad said—"I will ask Mr. Pradip to show you the house." He again pushed the call bell switch. Orderly again appeared.

"Call in Mr. Pradip."—Mr. Prasad ordered him.

"Yes Sir"—orderly responded bowing his head and went out.

Just after a few minutes a handsome young person entered the chamber asking "May I come in sir?"

'You are already in'—replied Mr. Prasad smilingly—"Meet Mrs. Prabha, She has joined today in our office. She needs a familial house where she may live comfortably. Actually she and her baby only are there to live in. I think even single bedroom house will do." He glanced towards me for my approval.

Mr. Pradip greeted me with folded hand. I too responded in the same manner and responded to Mr. Prasad—"Yes Sir, one bedroom will suffice if there is separate kitchen and toilet."

"There is a house in my locality. The house owner, Mr. Gupta, lives there with his family in the ground floor. A two—room flat is available on the first floor. The house owner had asked me for a renter a week before. During lunch break I will show the house to madam."—Mr. Pradip said politely.

"Is the house owner a good person? Mrs. Prabha is going to live there with his little son only."-Mr. Prasad asked pointing towards Ajju and gazing on Pradip's face.

"Don't worry for that sir. He is a nice man. He is busy with his shop right from seven in the morning to ten in the evening. His wife, one son and one daughter live with him. I know them personally. All the members of the family are very good and congenial. This boy will like the company of his daughter as she is very fond of children."—Mr. Pradip said courteously touching the cheeks of Ajju. Ajju first got hesitated but seeing smile on his face he too smiled.

"What is your name?—asked Pradip.

"Ajju"—replied Ajju

"Do you read"—Pradip asked.

"Yes"—Ajju replied boastfully.

"What do you read"—Pradip continued the questioning.

"A b c d and one two three four"—replied Ajju

"Good. Your are a very intelligent boy"—Pradip said Ajju looked towards me smilingly.

"O K then, you just explain her about dispatch and correspondence work and whenever you deem suitable let her show the house. It will be better to live in house than in a hotel. If house is ready to move Prabha should live there from very today. What is the use of paying room rent to hotel"—Mr. Prasad asked and indicated me to go with Mr. Pradip.

I came out of the chamber. Ajju was with me holding my finger. Mr. Pradip escorted me to a hall where there was arrangement to sit for six people. Four of the seats were occupied where two were vacant. Pradip asked me to sit on one of the vacant seats and sat on the other. He asked the peon to put extra chair for Ajju.

"Meet Mrs Prabha, she has joined today in our office".—Pradip told in announcing tone. Everyone looked at me. Pradip introduced with each of the members present there. "She is Kriti, Desk Officer"— He pointed to a lady who was sitting well dressed. Kriti just smiled and said—'hi'. I too responded. "He is Divyansu, Section officer, Shrinarayan Head Clerk and Usha Assistant. In this way he introduced with all the four persons present there and said—"and that is the chair which is meant for you." He indicated to the chair I was sitting on. He dragged the extra chair brought by the peon and said—"Here Baba will sit alongside his mom." He caught the hand of Ajju and made him sit at the chair. "Ramcharan, bring the dispatch box and register."—He spoke loudly seeing towards door. Ramcharan the peon came in and opened a almirah. He withdrew a small box and one long register. Pradip gave me a bunch of keys drawing from his drawer and told—"Here are keys of your drawer and dispatch box. There are some letters in the dispatch box. Just prepare envelopes and enter it in the register. Ramcharan will get it posted from nearby post office. This is the work at present. I will explain you the about other works.

But first we will go to meet Mr. Gupta to show you the house."

I started working. Ajju was a matter of interest for everyone. Whoever saw a little boy started talking with him. Ajju, responded to them in his lisping voice.

When dispatch work was complete I handed over the envelopes to Ramcharan and asked him to post them. Seeing this Pradip asked me to visit Mr. Gupta's house with him. He came out from the hall, went into the chamber of Mr. Prasad, perhaps to take permission from him to go outside. His bike was parked in one corner of the boundary of the office. He started his bike and asked me to sit on the pillion. I just sat made Ajju sit in between. After running of about one kilometer he stopped the vehicle in front of a shop. He introduced me with the shopkeeper, Mr. Gupta—"Madam has joined in my office and she is in search of a house. I think your house is still vacant. You have asked me one week ago to find a renter. I have found one for you."

"Mr. Gupta greeted me with folded hand and said to Pradip—"Ok, the house is still vacant. Let Madam first see the house and decide. My family members are present at home. You can go and see the house."

Pradip again started the bike and I sat on. Ajju was enjoying bike ride between us. Just after one furlong the bike turned to right side in a street. Although street was not very wide yet it was ok. Three houses were on the right side where as on the left side there were only boundaries. One house was on the last corner. The bike stopped there. There was a high boundary with strong steel gate. Pradip pushed the call bell push button. There was no response. "Perhaps electricity is gone"—He muttered and shouted in loud voice-"Pappu, Pappu."

A boy aged around sixteen came out and greeted Pradip—"good afternoon, uncle."

"Good afternoon Pappu. How are you?"

Pappu saw me with question mark on his face and responded Pradip—"I am fine, thank you uncle."

Seeing his approach towards me he introduced me—"She is Prabha auntie, she wants to hire your house. I have talked to your father. He has asked to see the house first. Is your mother inside home?"

"Namaste, auntie." He greeted me with folded hand. I replied nodding my head—"Namaste"

"Please come in."—He said and entered the house.

There was a good parking space in the boundary. On all sides just below the walls there were small vases in which different types of flowers were blooming. There was a small veranda and from it there was a stair to go upward. There were two doors one in front and another in left side. He entered from the front door and quickly opened the left side door and welcomed us to come in.

It was their living room. There was a sofa set in one side. To the right corner a big TV set was there. There was a couch on another side. Pappu indicated towards the sofa to seat on and went inside the house.

After a few minutes a lady came along with Pappu. She was a beautiful healthy lady of about forty five. She was Pappu's mother. Pappu had told the purpose of our visit to his mother. So she after greeting us invited us to come upstairs. She took Ajju in his lap. Ajju too went in her lap very comfortable.

"Why are you taking her in lap, he is now big enough to walk himself, and you will get tired going upstairs taking him in lap."—I told Mrs. Gupta.

"He is not so heavy."—She smiled.

We went upstairs. On the upper floor there was only one entrance unlike lower floor. It was from the front side. The left side entrance was not open on the upper floor. We entered the house. The first room was a big one. It would be better to call it hall rather than a room. With this hall there was a toilet to the right side. To the left side there was a kitchen. One more room was there just above the drawing room where we sat in the lower floor. The house was good one. Kitchen and bathroom all were decorated with good quality tiles and marbles. I liked the room very much. In fact it was not more than two kilometers from my office. For commuting from and to office it was suitable.

"I like it"—I told Mrs. Gupta—"but I have one problem, I would be in office from 10 to 4. I need one maid to look after Ajju. At least for two years I need a full time maid. At present Ajju is just four. He goes to play school only for three hours. When He will start going primary school a part time maid will do."

"That is not such a big problem. Just beside my house my maid lives. She will pleasantly do the job. In my house she washes the utensils and cleans the floor. She will have enough time to look after the baby."—She replied and turning to her son asked him to call the maid.

Pappu peeped from the window and called loudly—"Munni Ma"

"Ho"—a thin sound was heard

"Mother is calling you, please come."—Pappu said again

"Coming"—Munni Ma replied.

Within five minutes Munni Ma was present.

"She is going to live here"—Mrs. Gupta told indicating towards me—"She needs a maid to look after the baby and household chores. She will be in office from ten to four. Would you like to do the job?"

"I have no problem. But I will take one thousand rupees a month. After all it is a whole day business." She told as if she was justifying her demand of one thousand rupees wages.

"OK, I will give you one thousand rupees. I will be here from tomorrow"—I told her.

She looked satisfied. Perhaps she was expecting a bargain from me. May be she would have asked less money had she known that I would not bargain.

"Why from tomorrow? You have just to bring one or two suitcases from hotel. We can do it even at this moment."—Pradip said

"But I will have to manage for cots and utensils? I will manage it today and it will be proper to start living from tomorrow"—I replied.

"How many persons are you to live".-asked Mrs. Gupta.

"Just me and my son Ajju"—I replied.

"Then don't worry. Everything will be ready for you. Just go and bring your luggage. Munni Ma will clean the house well by the time you will be back. Whatever you would need take from me. Just return it when you purchase your own."-Mrs. Gupta assured me.

We returned to Mr. Gupta's shop. I told him that I liked the house and intended to hire it. He just said OK. When I asked about the rent he politely said that whatever I would pay he would accept.

At last it was finalized for Rupees two thousand a month. I calculated in my mind. One thousand for maid and two thousand for house rest four thousand will be enough for we mother and son. Pension will be credited in my bank account at Ranchi and in case of need it will be utilized.

We went direct to Hotel Seva. There I asked the counter clerk to clear my bill as I had to check out. Paying the bill we came outside. Waiter escorted us to the auto rickshaw. Luggage was kept in the auto rickshaw. I got in the auto rickshaw with Ajju. Pradip pointed the auto rickshaw driver where to go and started his bike.

When we reached the house it was really cleaned very well. One cot was also kept in the room. "I will send one table fan from my home. You keep it until you purchase ceiling fan"—Mrs. Gupta said. She added—"whatever your need please feel free to ask, I will provide it to you or arrange for it."

I was much happy finding such a cordial house owner and a good maid servant. I was very worried about where to live and how to manage while leaving Ranchi. But all went well. I intended to arrange the luggage but Pradip reminded me about office—"After four o clock you come from office and arrange the luggage." It was right. We were already out from office for more than one hour. When I went downstairs taking Ajju with me Munni ma asked me—"why are you taking baby with you? I will look after him." I looked towards Mrs. Gupta. She nodded her head in affirmation. Now I was feeling free. I handed over Ajju to Munni ma and instructed Ajju—"You stay here with auntie, I will return after some times." Ajju accepted it very easily as if he understood the problems of his mother. In fact from the very beginning he was living with me alone and was accustomed to live without me occasionally as there was none other than me to be with him.

I returned office with Pradip. He narrated me the correspondence works. I started working. In the meantime there was lunch hour. There was no question of lunch packet with me. Usha and Kirti requested me to take lunch with them. We took lunch and again started work. At four o clock when I was to leave office I went into the chamber of Mr. Prasad and took permission to leave he enquired about development of my residential arrangement. When I told him about Gupta's house he became satisfied. He too asked me that he is available for any type of help in case of need. Thanking him I returned.

I intended to take a rickshaw or auto rickshaw for my newly hired house but Pradip said that he lived in the same locality and he would escort me to the house. I came with him and thanked him for the favor.

"You are most welcome, please don't hesitate if you need any help from me"—saying so he turned his bike and went away.

"Look your mom has come."—hearing this sound I turned my neck towards the direction the sound was coming. Just to the left side of my house there was a hut. Munni ma was sitting there with Ajju. Looking me Ajju shouted—mamma, mamma. Munni ma lifted him in her arm and came to me. With her a little girl of about 11 was there. I did not feel difficulty in recognizing her as she resembled Munni ma.

"Is she your daughter?"—I asked to Munni ma

"Yes *malkin* she is my only daughter Munni." Munni ma responded.

"Now I understand why you are called Munni ma."—I said

She just smiled.

I went upstairs. Just after me Mrs. Gupta came with a girl. She introduced me with the girl—she is my daughter, Mithi. She is very fond of children. Ajju will like her companion.

Mithi took Ajju from my arms. Ajju seeing her smiling face went in her lap. She started talking with him and took him away.

"Mithi has taken Ajju away. Now you will find him only after an hour or two. Whenever she finds a baby she starts playing with it. By the way I have come to say you that your today's dinner will be with us."-Mrs. Gupta said.

"Why are you bothering yourself? We are only two people we will arrange for it."—I said overtly whereas I was feeling pleased as I had no arrangements for cooking food at that time.

"How will you arrange? You have no fuel to cook on. Although I will provide you one gas cylinder temporarily yet you start cooking from tomorrow, today you arrange your home as per your desire."—saying so she went downstairs.

Now I saw to my baggage. I was in a fix from where to start. For few minutes I could not decide what to do. But first of all I unpacked the baggage and started keeping items at proper place.

Munni ma came and asked me what to cook today. I told her that meal was being cooked in Mrs. Gupta's house. Again I told her that I would cook my food myself. She will have to clean the house and utensils and keep Ajju from ten to five.

"Where is Ajju Baba?—she asked.
I told her that he was with Mithi.
She returned.
Thus first day stay at Dumka was a pleasant stay.

12

From the second day I started my routine life. Whenever I was in need of something and Gupta family came to know about it they very merrily provided it to me. Gradually I was well settled there. Ajju was very much in demand among both Munni and Mithi. Pappu and Mr. and Mrs. Gupta too loved him much. They watched his every activity and he remained hot talk among them.

In office too I became familiar with my job. In fact the job was not very hectic nor was there much pressure. All colleagues were very helpful and cordial. Particularly Pradip was very helpful to all. That was the reason that he was much in demand from everyone in the office. Same was his fate in his neighborhood. Gradually layers of time faded the bitter memory of my divorce and demise of my parents. A normal life had begun. My world was confined in a closed circle in which along with Ajju, Munni Ma, Gupta family, Office colleagues were only members. No doubt among them Munni Ma and Pradip were having special status as they helped me a lot.

One morning when I awoke I felt body ache and fever. Due to weakness it was difficult to leave the bed. The wall clock was just after my sight. It was going to be seven. Ajju was lying beside me. He used to get up only when I left the bed. I was feeling much thirsty. Anyhow I awoke and took a glass of water and drank it. I did not have strength to stand or sit. Hence I once again lied down on the bed. There was a pat on the door by nine. I rose from the bed anyhow and unbolted the door and opened it. Munni Ma had come. Seeing my position she was surprised.

"What happened?" She asked.

"I am suffering from fever and body ache."—I told her moaning.

"She looked at me very sympathetically. Why did not you call me? You had just to give a call."—She told putting her palm on my forehead.

"It is too hot. You should contact a doctor."—She said worriedly. "Just take rest; I will bring some medicines from shop."

Hearing our talk Ajju just got up and asked for water. Munni Ma provided him a glass of water and called Munni loudly.

Within a moment Munni was present in school uniform. "Don't go to school today. You have to do some works here. You will have to look after Ajju for some hours. I will sweep the house and arrange for food and medicine for your auntie. She is sick."—Munni Ma instructed Munni.

Munni nodded her head in affirmative. She gave a sympathic look on me and took Ajju with her and went in the other room and started playing and talking with him.

I had employed Munni Ma only for cleaning utensils and sweeping of house, rest of works like cooking washing clothes I did myself. Today Munni Ma completed all the works without any direction from me. Again she forbid her daughter to go to school only to serve Ajju as she would be busy in doing household chores in my house and looking after me. I was feeling very thankful for her help.

She informed Mrs. Gupta about my illness. Mrs. Gupta came to see me. She consoled me to be worriless. She also arranged for paracetamol tablets from medicine shop. Munni Ma served me one piece of bread as having pill in an empty stomach would cause problem. I took one or two morsel of bread and swallowed the pill with the help of water. I again lied down on the bed. Within moments I was in the clutch of slumber.

When I awoke I felt nausea. It was so strong that I could not manage to get down from the bed. I just turned my head to save the bed from vomit and anyhow bowed down from the bed. A huge amount of vomiting was there. Munni Ma was sitting in the hall. Hearing vomiting sound she came inside. She put her hand gently on my head. Her hands were touching back side my neck very gently. When I comforted she brought a glass of water and asked me to rinse my mouth and drink water. I just rinsed and sipped mouthful of water. I once again lied down on the bed closing my eyes. The room has become untidy and stinking due to vomiting. It was worrying me. But what could I do. It was so abrupt that I could not manage to go to wash basin or bathroom.

Just after a few moments when I opened my eyes I saw that Munni Ma has cleaned the floor with phenyl very well. I was very much impressed by her quick and unasked service. Now I thought about Ajju. "Where is Ajju, Munni Ma?"-I asked in feeble voice.

"He is with Munni. Don't worry for Ajju. We will look after him. Your just take care of yourself:—she said smilingly—"Perhaps atmosphere of Dumka has not suited you so far."

In the meantime there was a sound of bike downward. Munni Ma peeped from the window and said—"*Bara Babu* from your office has come."

In the mean time Pradip entered the room and asked—"How are you? What is the position of fever?"

"I am fine. How did you come to know about my fever?"—I did not want to talk at that moment but any how I asked.

"I had telephoned Mr. Gupta when you did not reach office even by eleven. He told me about you. You too should keep a telephone connection or at least a mobile phone, it is very useful nowadays. Again it is not so costly now."—Pradip said.

Pradip extended his hand towards my forehead, perhaps to feel the temperature but stopped hesitatingly and said—"I will either call in a doctor or take you to doctor for check up."

"No, no! There are paracetamol tablets available in the house. I will be fine by tomorrow. Don't worry to go to doctor."—I said.

By this time Munni had come with Ajju. Ajju was surprised seeing me lying down in the bed. He could not understand what the reason was.

He asked—"Mamma is there holiday in my school. Why you did not you send me to school."

I replied in weak voice—"No my dear, there is no holiday but due to fever I could not get up in time and that's why could not send you school."

Nevertheless he was happy with Munni. Perhaps she took care for his every need and he was happy with her.

"We should not take medicine without consulting a doctor. It may cost heavily on the health. I will see what can be done."—saying so Pradip went downstairs. After some moments sound of starting of bike and departing could be heard.

"Munni, you just stay here and look after Ajju. I am going to home for taking bath. You sit near your auntie and provide her whatever she needs."

Munni sat on the floor and started playing with Ajju. Ajju was playing with his toy car and Munni was accompanying her. Only after one hour or so Munni Ma came and sat beside me. She touched my forehead to observe the fever. "It's too hot, it seems that the impact of the medicine is gone"—she exclaimed—"I am applying wet cloth on your forehead. It will help diminish fever."—saying so she went in the kitchen and brought a small bowl of water. She took a clean cloth piece. She just folded the cloth to make it handy, got it wet by dipping it in the bowl and put on my forehead. She repeated the process time and again. While doing so there was a splendid gesture on her countenance. It was full of love and affection. How helpful Munni Ma is. I thought. There is only a few—week acquaintance. Her duty is just to sweep the house and look after Ajju. But she cleaned the vomiting. She is nursing me without any request from me. There was some magic in her touch. I got drowsy and just slept within few minutes.

When I awoke after sometimes seeing Munni Ma I thought that my mother is sitting beside me. Finding me awoke she smiled. I wanted to call her Ma in lieu of Munni Ma. In fact she was serving me just like a mother does for her child.

In the meantime sound of motor car was heard. Munni Ma peeped from the window and informed me—"*Bara Babu* has come in a car". Pradip came upstairs and asked me to get ready as he had taken appointment with Dr Yadav. I asked her not to bother for me but he insisted for check up. At last I came downstairs. I saw that the car was our office car. How did you bring office car?—I asked.

"I was not bringing the office car. I had taken appointment with Dr. Yadav. He had assured to come with me in the evening. But when our boss knew that you are ill he offered me to take the car and go to the clinic of Dr. Yadav."—Pradip replied.

Dr. Yadav checked up me and declared that it is just viral fever and within one day or two it will go away. There is nothing to worry. He just prescribed a few medicines.

I returned home. Pradip escorted me home and returned.

The fever went out only next day however I was feeling weakness. The fever in the short span gave me a valuable message I have a mother like figure in Munni Ma and a very reliable and cordial friend in Pradip.

On the advice of Pradip I purchased a mobile phone. In fact it had become a necessity by that time and there was a mobile phone in every hand by that time. The first person I contacted over the phone was Harish Uncle as he was the only person in my contact from my old world.

13

In this way five years have been passed. Gradually memories of parents have been faded. There was no contact with old friends and relatives. There was communication with Harish uncle but it was decelerated by and by. With his help my house at Ranchi had been put on rent. The renter used to deposit rent in my account in the first week of the month.

Pradip had made a special place in my life. His helpful attitude had attracted me. When he came to know that I could not complete my studies due to various incidents he arranged for my studies from Open University. With his kind and timely help I could complete my studies. Bringing prospects, purchasing drafts, submitting assignments, filling in exam forms all were done with his help. As I completed graduation I was enthused to do further studies. So I just applied for post graduation course and it was near completion now.

I came to know that he was married to a girl who was a chronic heart patient. In those days there was little hope for heart patients particularly in the comparatively developing country like ours. "It is deemed inauspicious if a daughter dies unmarried"—Keeping this illusion in mind parents of that girl arranged her marriage with Pradip hiding the fact of her unceasing heart disease. After marriage the girl narrated the situation to Pradip. Though being cheated, Pradip tried his best to keep her happy as it was clear that she is not going to live for more than a year. More over it was her father who was responsible for hiding the fact and not she. As they belong from rural background there was no question of acquaintance between them before marriage.

Whenever she walked a few steps she started panting badly. Due to her bad health their marriage was never consummated. Within six to seven months his wife died in his arms. While dying she apologized from Pradip on part of her parents telling that she did not want to cheat him but could not do anything against the will of her parents. Again she had requested Pradip to get married soon after her death. But this incident had devastating impact on Pradip's mind. He never thought of marriage after that. He seldom goes to his home as all these bitter memories would disturb there. All these stories were being narrated to me by my colleagues Kriti and Usha. Again Mrs Gupta too explained me this sad story.

But after meeting with me his mind was changed to some extent. During exchange of views he had expressed his idea about marriage and remarriage. In his opinion widow marriage or marriage with a divorced was not only acceptable but most welcome. He had quoted an example of a T V actress who had been divorced by his drunkard tramp husband. She had a five year old daughter who lived with her after divorce. Another colleague actor had accepted to marry her and accept her daughter. While quoting this his eyes were hovering on my face observing meticulously my feelings and reactions. Perhaps he was trying to guess my viewpoint and my reaction in the matter.

His view on remarriage attracted me too. May I remarry with anyone? I had never thought in such a way before. In fact there was no divorce case in my family or relatives. There were a few cases of widowhood. But no widow had been remarried in the history of my family or relatives. But a few cases of widow marriage or abandoned marriage have occurred in recent years in the society. Hearing such discussions I contemplated whether I should marry again. After all I am not so old. I am only in my thirties. Then keeping in view the changing scenario in the society should I marry with anyone? And why anyone, Pradip was expressing his views to know my opinion. Recitation of TV actress case and emphasizing acceptance of daughter by her would be husband was perhaps indication from him that he would like to marry me and accept Ajju. But he never expressed his views clearly. I too was in a dilemma. From whom could I take advice? And god knows all that I was thinking may be only what I think and not the true picture. Pradip would have discussing the matter just in normal course.

But I could not stop myself from comparing us both. His wife had left the world. It was beyond her control to stay with him. After marriage she must have been impressed by Pradeep. Even being cheated by his in laws he never mistreated his wife. Rather he tried to keep her happy. So she must have wanted to live with such generous husband a full life. And why only full life, the next seven lives. After all couple commit to live together seven lives in marriage rituals.

My husband had left my world. It was within his control to stay with me. The only corrective measure that he needed to take was to shed off his skeptic behavior, to put off the deceit of being male, being husband. He had relinquished me for no fault from my part. It is true that I had a lot of reverence and love for him in my early married life which he dried up by his skeptic and haughty behavior.

We both, I and Pradip, were in the same circumstances. If we match with each other problems of both of us will be solved. We both will get a life partner. The understanding that we were showing and feeling in last few years is sufficient to indicate that we will be an ideal couple. Ajju will get full parentage. Had Pradip desired so he may get his own son or daughter from me.

But there was society who will not accept divorcee remarriage, then what about the society? How society will react when we marry and start conjugal life. I was thinking of society that was never useful for me. This society never extended its helping hand towards me. The society treated me and my family as untouchable only because I was a divorced, that too for no fault on my part. Although not declared clearly but our family was almost excommunicated by the society after my divorce. My near and far relatives became quite alien to me. Due to the attitude of the society I lost my mother first and thereafter my father. After death of my parents no one except Harish uncle helped me. The director tried to delay my appointment and asked for sexual pleasure for local posting. Still I was thinking of that cruel and insensitive society. The society has tied the man, his emotions, in an invisible thread.

Even if I accept the offer of Pradip what will be my condition thereafter? What will be the future of Ajju. Will Pradip be able to provide Ajju fatherly affection? Or will it be only affectation? Particularly when there would be another issue from me after our conjugal life would Pradip be able to equally love both Ajju and new born baby? For me both would be my own offspring but for Pradip Ajju will perhaps remain alien. Would not he discriminate against Ajju and his own son or daughter? Moreover will Ajju accept Pradip as his father from the bottom of his heart?

There was two continuous sound of hitting on the electric pole just below our house. It was two in the morning. The night watchman used to move in entire locality with a torch and a strong bamboo cane in his hand. He used to strike the poles number of times proportionately to indicate the time. I looked to the clock. It was quarter past two. The morning incident had so much exasperated me that I could not sleep even after two in the morning whereas I was habituated to sleep by eleven. "I must sleep now"—I thought and turned side. Ajju was fast asleep. After some moments I slept but very lightly. There were incoherent dreams throughout.

That was the end of diary. It covered a large part of my life. But a few later chapters of my life remained still uncovered. I watched the clock. It was one afternoon. Ajju must have been coming. He prefers rice and *rajma* curry. I should cook it first. If the lunch is not ready on his return home Ajju gets annoyed. On other days I keep lunch ready in fridge. But on holidays I cook it in such a way that hot lunch is available to consume. I cooked rice in a pot and put *rajma* in pressure cooker.

Again my mind travelled to Dumka and I tried to recollect the parts of my life that was not covered in the diary . . . .

Ultimately I got up in the morning at six and awoke Ajju. I made him ready for school. When school-rickshaw came he went to school.

In the meantime Munni Ma came for completing household chores. Now she used to do household works in the morning. Her duty started in the evening when Ajju returned from school till my return from office. When Munni Ma looked at my face she became worried. "What happened? Why your eyes are swollen? Are you sick? Should I send message to *Bara Babu?*"— So many questions at a time.

I looked at her with love in my eyes. How much she cares for me. I replied-Nothing Munni Ma, I could not sleep well yesterday."

"Why? Is there any problem?"—She questioned me.

"No, no there is no problem. It happens sometimes. Don't worry at all Munni Ma"—I assured her.

Getting assurance she started sweeping the floor. I started glancing over the paper but today no news or column could attract me. My head and eyes were heavy. To some extent I felt feverish. I wished to take a cup of tea. Normally I do not take tea in the morning but at that moment I was feeling need of tea. So I prepared tea and giving one cup to Munni Ma started sipping. Every now and then picture of that beggar couple appeared in my mind. Viraj too was encroaching into my mind many times. In between came Pradip. Viraj was a distressed past and Pradip a pleasant present. Pradip may be a pleasant future too—I thought.

After some time I got ready and went to office. I started my work. Pradip too was present beside my seat. I have noticed he watched me every now and then stealthily. I too got attracted toward him gradually. If Pradip proposes me I will accept it—I thought. But perhaps Pradip did not gather enough courage to express his love explicitly.

The days were passing. I waited for his proposal as I had made up my mind to marry him. After all we both were sufferer of misfortune. His wife had left the world due to physical illness. My husband had left my world due to his mental bug. His wife could not escape the fate. My husband did not shun his skeptic and cynic nature. Due to demise of his wife he was alone in the world. Due to retreat of my husband I was alone in the world. Thus we both were in same predicament. Joining with each other would mitigate the hardship of both of us. Ours may be a happy and merry life.

After a few days it happened so one day that boss ordered me and my colleague Sanjay to go to Dhanbad for some official work. There was a workshop organized by our head office. Boss narrated us details of the project and advised to give our presentation in emphatic way. Staff members were coming there from every corner of state. I was worried for Ajju. Although Munni Ma looked after him very well during day when I was in office and now he is sufficiently grown up yet I had never left him alone going out of station. So I was worried. I requested boss to depute someone else telling him reason of my anxiety. Boss expressed his inability to do anything in the matter. In fact in past whenever such situation occurred boss had managed accordingly. But perhaps this time he was unable to do me favor because many staff members were on leave and some had gone out of station on deputation. So ultimately I had to go to Dhanbad along with Sanjay.

We left Dumka early in the morning as we had to reach Dhanbad by ten o'clock. Office car had been provided to us. The workshop started in time but as there was a hectic program it took a long time and we could be freed only after seven in the evening. During the seminar we had been asked to switch off our mobiles. When I switched on my mobile after meeting was over I found many missed calls from Pradip. I called him back. The ring went on but nobody answered. I rang again and again anxiously worrying that there may be some news for Ajju but he did not pick up the phone. At last I contacted with Mrs. Gupta and knew about Ajju.It was more than four hour running from Dhanbad to Dumka. We reached by eleven o clock. The driver dropped me first and went away with Sanjay.

When I reached home Ajju was still awoke with Munni Ma. "I tried my best to make him sleep but could not."—Munni Ma said laughingly—"I have told him at least five stories".

"Mamma, I can't sleep without you. I don't feel well when you are not near me."—Ajju exclaimed boisterously. It touched my emotion. "Poor boy, it was first time in his life when I was away from him at bed time."—I thought but said overtly—"Now you are a grown up and a student of high school. Munni Ma takes care of you very well. Why can't you sleep?"

The next day when I reached office Pradip was present on his seat. He always used to greet me warmly but today he pretended as if he had not noticed me come. I greeted him—"Namaskar Pradipji. How are you?"

"I am fine."—Pradip replied sternly. He did not raise his head and kept himself busy over the register.

"You did not receive my call yesterday? I tried many times to connect your mobile."—I asked.

"I may be busy."—He replied unsympathetically.

"But when you saw missed call later you should have called me back."—I asked

"I am busy in some work please don't disturb me. I will talk later about it."—He told coldly.

I was surprised. He never talked so roughly to anyone. He was always sympathetic to me. I could not understand what the matter was. Although I started working yet my mind was tangled in his harsh behavior. Earlier whenever I called him on his mobile phone and he could not respond at the moment he called me back whenever got time. Yesterday he did not call me back and when I asked about it he just avoided it.

I started contemplating. Pradip is such a generous person. He takes care of all. He never misbehaves anyone. With me he was so friendly until yesterday, not yesterday the day before yesterday, and then what went wrong abruptly? What happened in one day that is yesterday that changed his mood so drastically? I had gone to Dhanbad for official work and was in meeting. My mobile phone was switched off so I could not receive his call. Just after meeting was over I called him back and resentfully he did not respond. He did not even ask me why I could not answer his call.

The reason was becoming clearer now. I had gone with Sanjay to Dhanbad. He did not like my going with Sanjay. But what could I do. It was official order. Had boss ordered me to go alone I had to obey it. Had I been ordered to go with Pradip I should have obeyed it. But what may be the reason of his not liking my going with Sanjay. Perhaps he was jealous with Sanjay. Or perhaps he had become over possessive about me. Why he is so possessive. What right he has over me to be so possessive. No doubt he helps me a lot. But does his helping attitude provide him authority on me.

Today I have gone with Sanjay. Tomorrow I may go with someone else if situation warrants so. Then he will again react in the same way. And I am pondering over about marriage with him. What if after marriage I will have to go outside with some male member for official work. And why outside what if I talk with a male colleague in office for official work.

This tour program had revealed another face of Pradip. His behavior has been exposed by it.

I looked towards Pradip. It appeared that Viraj's and Pradip's face has been intermingled. Viraj was my husband and then he was skeptic. Pradip is none for me at present except a colleague. Even then he turned a cynic only knowing that I have gone outside with some person and that too for office work. He did not bother how hectic our program was. He did not enquire why my mobile phone was switched off and why I could not respond to his call.

Would such person be a suitable match for me? Would not he suspect me every now and then? Would not he prove to be another Viraj for me? Would not my heart be broken by Pradip in whose inner mind another Viraj was living?

I would not accept the marriage proposal from Pradip. I had seen another Viraj in him. And what to talk about Pradip, I would not think of marriage at all in my life. Not with any one however helpful and sympathetic he may appear. My only aim is now to educate Ajju well and make him self-dependant. I need nothing more from my life. Whatever I have received from my life till now is more than enough.

Ding dong . . . . Ding dong . . . . Hearing sound of call bell I just came to the present world from my past. I unbolted the door. Ajju came in.

What were you doing Mom? I have rung the call bell many times and cooker is blowing whistle for a long time. What are you cooking? Ajju said keeping his bag on the table and again staring at the screen of his mobile and fiddling with the keyboard of mobile set. I rushed in the kitchen and switched off the stove.